MW01173520

Grind Show Editions

BOY HERO

Michael Joseph Walsh was born on January 13, 1960 in Buffalo, New York of Irish, German, and Italian ancestry.

Walsh was a rebellious and adventurous youth, leaving Minneapolis for Florida at nineteen. He hitchhiked frequently, and journeyed to San Diego, California soon after he turned twenty. He resided in California for eighteen years; also living in Sacramento and the San Francisco Bay Area.

In 1995, Walsh graduated "with distinction" from California College of Arts and Crafts in Oakland. The following year he created the book titled *Graffito*, a photo documentary of the graffiti phenomenon in San Francisco. The book was well received in the US and Europe.

Walsh ventured to Prague, Czech Republic in 1997 and began a body of work titled *Frontier Town*, which explores the remnants of Soviet communist rule and occupation in Prague. For the next year he traveled the city extensively by tram and subway with his camera.

In 1998, his work in Prague was cut short when he was awarded a Fulbright Scholarship in Photography to Taiwan. That fall Walsh arrived in Taipei and began work on a capacious photo essay of Taiwanese culture titled *Shangri-la Motel* (unpublished). In 2011, *Cadillac Fin Suitcase* was published, a collection of short stories set in Taiwan. He lived in Taiwan for ten years.

Western Roads was published in 2013; a semiautobiographical tale that follows Walsh and his friend Othello Bolen, who flee Minneapolis to California after a violent incident in St. Paul.

Also by Michael Walsh

Graffito
Cadillac Fin Suitcase
Western Roads

BOY HERO is a Grind Show Editions book
In association with The Truxton 5

BOY HERO is a work of fiction. All characters appearing in this work are fictitious. Any resemblance to real persons, either alive or dead, is purely coincidental.

Copyright © 2016 by Michael Walsh
All rights reserved. This complete work is registered with the US Copyright Office. No part of this book may be reproduced in any form or by any electronic or mechanical means, including information storage and retrieval systems without permission in writing from the author, except by a reviewer, who may quote brief passages in a review.

ISBN-13: 978-0-692-60153-2   ISBN-10: 0-692-60153-8

For my family

March 4, 2016
Dave & Kathy,
Your love and support
have been awesome!
Thank you!
thank you!
Mike

Boy Hero

Mr. Hai Lee was in delirium.

Boyhood scenes blazed behind closed eyes as he sat in a rocker on his *san-ho yuan's* porch. His face a red clay field furrowed with tiger paths.

Hai Lee's malady had worsened in recent months—always a different and distressing version of the same wartime memory settling upon him, its climax usually causing nausea.

Delirium ebbed to despair after a half hour. Hai Lee's eyes opened and slowly brightened at the triumphant mango orchard before him. He ran a hand over a white T-shirt and black mud-caked work shorts that clung to his sinewy frame.

He stood up, strode across the red-tiled courtyard into the orchard. He put an ear to the base of a tree—imagined hearing a heartbeat. He sprung up and danced around ecstatically—his passion cresting to bliss. He lifted his arms toward the blue and pink sky, and meditated upon rising puffy clouds.

Hai Lee about faced and admired his san-ho yuan's u-shape, red brick walls and elegant sloping tile roof. The tiles shone like imperial topaz as twilight neared.

A single strand of incense smoke curled out between the two red wooden front doors, which were swung open completely and gave the appearance of the wings of an exotic butterfly. Above the door hung five hand-painted yellow lanterns, protecting the home from spirits of the underworld.

Hai Lee returned to his rocker and sat down. He again marveled at his mango trees. He owned five hectares (2.5 acres = 1 hectare). Five fallow hectares stretched out behind the dwelling.

At seventy-two, people said Hai Lee was the best mango grower in Southern Taiwan—a bigoted benevolent son of a bitch.

Hai's eyes lifted and he gazed with awe at the emerald fields of the Ciatou countryside that fell off the Earth. His mind strayed to his late wife, and he thought of the black-and-white photograph of them that sat in a gilded frame on his dresser. His eyes hardened a bit and his mouth became dry and tight.

Flashing lights momentarily appeared in the edges of his vision as they had several times recently.

"Are these damn lights and the memory episodes connected?" he growled. "No," he concluded, "never happens at the same time."

Hai Lee rubbed his eyes, reached into a plastic bag in

his shirt pocket, pulled out a betel nut, and popped the fleshy green nut into his mouth. Betel nut is the seed of the areca palm, Taiwan's second leading agricultural crop. It buzzes your top like chewing tobacco.

A Toyota sedan with a wake of brown dust stormed up the narrow dirt road that ran along the right side of the mango orchard from the main road.

The car stopped abruptly in front of the san-ho yuan. A rangy teenage boy got out of the passenger side and stood uneasily in the dirt road.

He wore a new pair of white Adidas, Levi's blue jeans, and a dark blue T-shirt. A brown suitcase trembled slightly in the boy's hand. He squinted and held up the other hand to shield his eyes from the setting sun.

Hai Lee stood up as tall as he could, straightened his shoulders and muttered to himself, "She hates me. But you need me now, don't you, you old sucker fish?"

The car quickly pulled away. The old man stared silently at the boy.

"Uh, hello, Grandpa!" the boy called out. He walked gingerly into the red tiled courtyard as if it were a minefield.

"Damn strawberry," grumbled the frowning old man, and he looked the boy up and down and spit a stream of betel-nut juice that landed, a red splotch, between him and the boy.

"You look pretty as a poodle."

The boy was shocked. "That's what you have to say, Grandpa, after not seeing me since I was nine? Everybody calls me Curtis now."

"You call me 'Grandfather' or 'sir,' or I'll plant you with the mangos," the old man grunted and grabbed a yellow pack of Long Life cigarettes from his shirt pocket, flicked one of the butts into his mouth and lit it with a butane lighter. "What the hell's wrong with your real name? Why some fool foreigner name?"

"A lot of people have English names now."

"Well, you're Strawberry to me."

The boy pouted knowing "Strawberry" was derogatory, meaning to be soft or weak, used by elders to describe the boy's generation, who've had the fortune of growing up in more prosperous times.

"Set that monkey box down and hold out your hands."

"What for?" the boy asked meekly.

"Palms up, Straw Boy."

The boy set the suitcase down at his side and held his hands out in front of his grandfather.

The old man didn't look at the boy's hands. He gave the boy a hard stare, turned his head, spit a splotch of betel-nut juice that nicked the boy's shoe, and muttered with disgust, "Delicate as lotus blossoms."

"So," the boy whispered under his breath, and he looked dejectedly at the red stain on his pristine shoe.

The old man sat down in his chair and said, "You'll get your badges starting tomorrow morning."

"Badges?"

The iPhone in the boy's hip pocket began to ring.

"Take a seat," commanded the old man, ignoring the boy's question.

The boy took out his iPhone and said, "Hello?"

The old man sprang out of his chair, grabbed the iPhone out of the boy's hand, looked at it and spat, "We had no telephone when I was a boy. Thanks to Chiang-kai Shek we got one radio station—Radio Coolie," and he shoved the iPhone into his own pocket and sat down.

The boy shrugged indifferently.

"Take a seat!" growled the old man. "This ain't aunty's. I bet she cussed me the whole ride over."

"Nothing wrong with her a gallon of gas and a match couldn't fix," said the boy and he sat in the cane chair across from his grandfather.

"That's raw, kid." The old man eyed the boy with suspicion. "How old are you now?"

"Fourteen."

"You looked a helluva lot more promising at your parents' funeral."

"So did you." The boy looked scared, even as he said it.

"Your aunt told me you're a delinquent," scolded the old man, not letting on that he liked the boy's retort. "Extorting money from a girl at school with a group of thugs. Terrorizing a girl? True?"

The boy bowed his head in shame, looked at the timeworn red tile beneath his feet, and shifted uneasily in the chair. He felt hot.

"They forced me to or they said they'd, uh—"

"Damn it all, Straw Boy! You've disgraced our family name! What kind of punks are you going around with?"

The boy continued to look down.

"Your precious aunt said you're fit to work. And that's what you're going to do here all summer until school starts. Then back to her if she'll take you. Screw up the government will own you until you're eighteen. Put you in a foster home with some freak."

The boy peeked up at the old man with forlorn eyes.

"Your aunt said you're a TV addict, too."

"She's lying."

"Uh huh." The old man's eyes screwed into the boy's, and he said casually, "There's no TV here. No computer. Work hard and you'll earn access to my library. F off you can mummify for all I care."

Dread rippled through the boy as he tried to imagine life without TV.

The old man stuck his jaw out and said, "I suppose you're feeling sorry for yourself because of what happened to your parents. You better learn to take it boy, because life ain't a bowl of cherries. You're not the only one. I lost my wife five years ago, and my only child, your sweet mother in that god-awful accident."

The boy's parents tumbled in his mind. Broken. Bloody. Beatific.

"Will I get an allowance?" the boy finally said.

The old man laughed mockingly. "Cons don't get paid," he said, shaking his head. "You've got five hundred hours with me for what you did to that girl. And I hear you're getting cruddy grades, too. Are you stupid, is that it?"

He didn't give the boy a chance to answer. "You're going to get worked to death, boy! You're going to work and work until all that silly crap is leached out of your damn bones!"

"Silly crap," the boy mimicked under his breath.

"I'm the big bug around here, kid," the old man shot wrathfully. "The king bee. Meanest sting in the county. And I can eat strawberries all day long."

He stood up and walked into the house. "I'll never bleed the nonsense out of this kid, wife," the old man said, and he opened a drawer in the kitchen and pulled out a pair of electric clippers.

He returned with the clippers and a white towel, which he threw around the unsuspecting boy's shoulders.

"What are you doing, you crazy old man?!" the boy yelled with fright.

When he tried to rise, the old man held him lightly, easily in place.

"You go to work tomorrow. You look like a damned girl with this Japanese devil's hairdo. You don't want a dog or some convict on the lam to come along and hump you, do you?"

The boy squirmed when the old man turned on the clippers. The old man grabbed one of the boy's ears and twisted it hard as he began shearing the back of his head. Five minutes later, the job was complete. The boy whimpered as he ran his hands over his shaved head.

"Why did you want a Japanese dog haircut, anyway?" asked the old man as he quickly ran the clippers over his own shorn scalp.

"It's the style," said the boy plainly, trying to conceal his humiliation.

"Don't they teach you your own history?" said the old man in disgust.

He shook his fist and continued, "Those Japanese devils enslaved us for fifty years. Made me learn their damn language. Beat me in school if I spoke my native tongue. Forced our young women into becoming comfort women."

"It's 2007. That was a long time ago."

"It was yesterday."

The old man turned off the clippers. "Clean up this mess, Strawberry, and come in for supper."

The old man walked into the house muttering, "It was yesterday. It's today. It's every damn day."

2

The old man woke at five thirty the following morning. It was raining hard. This pleased him as he put on black cotton work pants, a white T-shirt, and calf-high rubber boots. At 5:45 the old man appeared at the boy's door.

"Breakfast," the old man barked, and headed toward the kitchen.

The rain stopped. The sun appeared. Sullen. Resolute. The soul without a soul.

After a quick meal of rice soup and egg sandwiches, the old man threw the boy a pair of old work pants, rubber boots, a wide-brimmed bamboo hat, and a white T-shirt with the word "hoodlum" scrawled in Chinese characters across the front with felt-tip marker.

"I'm not wearing this," exclaimed the boy as he examined the T-shirt.

"That's what you are."

"I told you I didn't really—"

"You'll wear it every day in the fields until I tell you it doesn't fit you any more, if that ever happens. You should feel lucky. In my day they might have tattooed it across your chest."

Reluctantly, the boy stripped off his blue T-shirt. The old man stared in horror at the boy's chest and abdomen—at least fifteen long scars, some fresh red lines, others much older crisscrossed the torso. The old man knew the boy wasn't in the accident that killed his parents.

The old man said, "What happened?"

The boy didn't answer.

"Punks you running with do that?"

"No."

"Who, dammit?"

"I did it."

"You?" The old man shook his head in disbelief. "Put on that 'hoodlum' shirt."

The boy put on the "hoodlum" shirt, hastily donned the rest of the clothes and followed his grandfather to a traditional Taoist family ancestral shrine that occupied the small room inside the front door.

The walls and wood-beam ceiling were smoked a deep reddish brown from decades of burning incense. Taoists believe the incense smoke carries their prayers to the spirits of gods and ancestors. A twelve-foot-wide mahogany altar spanned the back wall. A small wooden statuette of the goddess Kuanyin—her head and face blackened by years of smoke, sat in the center of the altar.

To Taoists, Kuanyin is the goddess of mercy. They believe that faithful prayer to her will assist in facing any problem.

Offerings of snacks—pineapple, mango, and banana—lay in front of her. These offerings were gifts for her and for departed ancestors. A vase of lilies and a vase of orchids sat at either end of the long table.

The old man was a devout Taoist, praying at the altar each day. He took great pride in tending to the shrine, changing the offerings often and making sure at least one stick of incense was always burning.

The old man lit six sticks of incense and handed three to the boy. They knelt down in front of the altar and prayed in silence. The boy had forgotten some of the prayer rituals, and he waited for the old man to raise the incense in front of his face and wave it forward three times before mimicking him.

The old man stood up and placed the incense in a small urn that sat in front of Kuanyin. Again, the boy followed his grandfather's movements exactly.

Without uttering a word, the old man walked outside, grabbed the wide-brimmed bamboo hat that hung on the wall beside the front door, put it on, and marched through the courtyard and around the side of the house toward a shed attached to a small barn fifty meters away.

The boy followed, chewing a fingernail. He coldly scanned the countryside. Few puddles remained from the torrent an hour earlier.

Out here, northwest of the clamor of Kaohsiung City, flatlands exploding with rice, cabbage, cauliflower, and sugar cane flowed out to the sanctuary of Matsu, goddess of the sea, as the sun, brutal and unrelenting now, rolled over the landscape.

The betel-nut-chewing old man came out of the shed leading a white bull by a long thin rope. He used his other hand to balance a wooden plow on his shoulder.

"You didn't jack off last night, did you?" said the old man and spat a splotch of betel nut juice.

"No!"

"Do it in the john or outside. I don't want to be washing your sheets all the damn time."

The boy was too embarrassed to reply.

"I suppose you've never worked an honest day in your life have you?"

"I'm in school."

"School's school. It ain't work. Oh hell, school's all right. But you kids get too much of it. Problem with you strawberries is that the whole damn society coddles and wet nurses you kids 'til you're not worth a damn. Parents pamper and wipe your asses. We got a whole stinking nation of computer game addicts with the attention span of a flea that at twenty-two years of age after college haven't worked one day in their lives, not one day, and have never earned a dollar."

"What about when you were a kid?" the boy asked, following his grandfather toward the fields and looking sideways nervously at the bull.

The old man ignored the boy's question. "Mr. Shih in town owns a motorcycle repair shop—he's a smart one—has two boys about your age, and he's taught them how to work. One of them goes to high school in the day and works at the shop at night, and the other works at the shop during the day and goes to school at night. They run the place by themselves half the time. Real fine young men—polite, courteous, hell they're years beyond you, kid."

"What about you?"

"I was working in the fields right alongside my mother and father when I was seven. And it was work, boy, ten, twelve hours a day or we didn't eat. We were bent over all day long working a shovel or a hoe—no one ever saw our faces. When I was eighteen I did my mandatory three-year hitch in the Army. Nowadays, you pansies are only required to do thirteen puny months."

"Did you have to fight?"

"It was peacetime in the mid 1950s. You don't pay attention at school, do you dim-wit?"

The boy winced as if stung by the remark. "What about your school?"

"Some," said the old man, and he stopped next to a barren patch of ground and dropped the plow. "I made it to the fourth grade. My dad taught me how to read and write."

He dug the plow into the rich black earth, bent down, grabbed a handful of the moist soil, and said, "Hold out your lotus blossoms."

"What?"

"Hold out your damn hands!"

The boy held out his hands. The old man placed the soil into the boy's cupped hands, and the boy held it without appreciation.

"What's that for?"

"Smell it."

"Why?"

"Go on."

The boy lifted his hands to his face and smelled the soil. "I don't get it," he shrugged.

The old man gazed at the boy for a long moment.

"You're in paradise and don't even know it. Not my place, but here," and the old man spread his arms wide, turned and swept them toward the countryside. "You're full of cement and plastic," then he bent down and hooked up the plow to the bull and stood behind it.

"Now pay attention, boy," he said, "so when it's your turn that old bull won't kick you to Saigon."

The old man set the tongue of the plow into the earth with his foot, gently flicked the long rope, and he and the bull began to walk slowly and gracefully along the empty field. Every few meters the old man flicked the rope so that it barely brushed up against the bull's side.

The old man and the bull plowed fifty meters, turned around, and plowed back a parallel row one meter over from the first run.

"Your turn," said the old man, and he handed the rope to the boy and reached in his shirt pocket for his cigarettes.

The boy fumbled and stuttered along during his first run. His grandfather walked behind him barking out instructions. It was slow work. At eight the harsh sun was brazing the backs of their necks. By ten the boy and the bull had plowed five crooked rows with the old man watching from the shade of a tree.

While they were plowing the sixth row the old man's thoughts drifted to the scars on the boy's torso. He became frightened. He remembered hearing about a local boy who'd mutilated his arms in a similar fashion.

"I don't have whatever the hell I need to help this boy," he fretted. "What am I going to do? What the hell's wrong with him?"

Around noon, the old man cupped a hand around his mouth and called out, "Lunch time, Strawberry."

The boy's sweat-covered shoulders dropped. "Okay," he said.

The old man stood up and walked over to the boy.

"After lunch you're going to plant some corn."

"Corn?"

"What the hell do you think we've been doing here all morning? This is your cornfield, boy. You plowed it. You're going to plant it. You're going to tend it. And you're going to pick it. And you're going to cook it. I suppose you don't know how to cook, either?"

"Not really."

"Add that one to your list."

"Are we going to eat the corn, too?" the boy asked meekly.

"Damn right. Now you take that animal into the barn and make sure he's got plenty of water. When you're done, come on up to the house."

"Okay," said the boy, and he led the bull to the barn.

After lunch the old man taught the boy how to plant corn by hand in the twelve rows they'd plowed in the morning.

The boy worked hard next to his grandfather in the hot sun. At three the planting was done.

"Come on hoodlum," said the old man, and he walked toward the mango orchard without looking at the boy.

Curtis followed his grandfather into the orchard. The old man walked slowly in the short grass in between a row inspecting the trees. He reached out his hand and brushed it against many of the impressive Chin-huang mangos that hung down on long vines.

The boy mimicked his grandfather's every move as he walked behind at a safe distance.

The old man stopped, climbed a step-ladder that was under one of the trees, and said, "Get the other ladder and get your butt up here."

"I don't see it."

"It's next to a mango tree."

"Smart ass," said the boy under his breath.

He scanned the orchard, then he ran and retrieved the other ladder, set it down next to his grandfather's, and climbed up so that his eyes were level with the old man's. The boy looked around at the multitude of hefty greenish-yellow mangos.

The old man gently cupped one of the fruit in his hand, leaned over, smelled it and said, "Abroad they call these beauties 'Golden Queens.' I know what you need honey," he said softly, smiled, and let go of the mango. "Try it."

The boy reached out, roughly grabbed one of the mangos, and yanked it hard toward his face causing the branch to creak.

"Son of a bitch," said the old man. "Careful, boy. These are the bosoms of goddesses—our goddesses."

"Sorry."

"Try again."

The boy reached out, took a different mango in his hand, leaned over and smelled it.

"Give you a hard-on?" asked the old man.

"No."

"It will, if you ever wise up."

"When will they be ready to pick?"

"Know why these are so special?" asked the old man ignoring the boy's question.

"Why?"

"They're virgins—one hundred percent organic. There's never been a drop of chemical in this orchard. Harvest is from early July through August, usually. It depends on the weather, the rain, and how many typhoons wallop us." He climbed down the ladder and walked toward the barn. "Wait here," he shouted over his shoulder.

He returned ten minutes later with a plastic two-gallon spray bottle with a long hose and nozzle. He strapped the spray bottle onto his back. The boy followed his grandfather as he headed twenty meters down a row and stopped, set up a nearby ladder, climbed to the top, and began spraying a clear liquid onto the mangos.

"What's that for?" asked the boy.

"It's a family secret. A special herbal concoction with fish amino acid that your great-great grandfather conjured up with the help of Kuanyin. It makes these darlings grow bigger and taste sweeter. You've got to promise me to guard our secret with your life, if I'm ever dumb enough to give it to you."

"I promise."

"A few of the other growers use chemical pesticides."

"Why?"

"They're lazy. Hell, that's like rubbing down an infant with turpentine after its bath. Did you notice the curry shrubs planted around the perimeter, and how clean and weed-free the orchard is?"

"Yeah, I guess," the boy said indifferently and shrugged

his shoulders.

The old man scowled at the boy's disinterest. "The curry ain't for show," he growled. "They attract insects that will kill off most insect pests. And weeds attract all kinds of destructive bugs."

For the rest of the afternoon, under his grandfather's direction, the boy lopped off several stray branches, cultivated around the perimeters of trees with a hoe, and pulled weeds that had recently sprung up in the otherwise clean, dark soil.

At four the boy rested his hoe against his shoulder, wiped his sweaty brow, and inspected several large blisters on his palms and fingers. His grandfather took notice and walked up to the boy, who quickly got back to work with the hoe.

The old man grabbed the hoe away from the boy with one hand, and one of the boy's hands with the other and said sarcastically, "Congratulations Straw Boy. You've been officially deflowered. Better get used to those badges, because besides chow and a bunk, they're the only thing you're going to get around here unless you get wise and learn how to see."

The boy gave him a quizzical look and asked, "See what?"

"Between the winds," said the old man, and he walked away.

At around five the boy brooded as he worked the hoe.

Guilt and self-loathing from extorting money from the girl at school consumed him, keeping the healing powers of the land and sky and trees at bay.

The old man was working from a ladder twenty meters away. He was pleased with the boy's progress and work ethic, but he didn't let that on to the boy. They continued to work and knocked off at six.

"Follow me, Straw Boy," said the old man as he walked toward a meter-tall mound of graves in the rear right corner of the property, 200 meters from the san-ho yuan.

In Taiwan it's not custom for a grave site to be located on private property. It's considered bad luck to enter a cemetery except for a burial or on Tomb Sweeping Day; a national holiday in early April, in which many families visit ancestral graves to honor the dead and rid the graves of overgrown grass and weeds. Neighbors protested long ago, and asked that the graves be moved to a public cemetery, but Mr. Hai Lee's father and grandfather paid them no mind.

The boy ran to catch up to his grandfather, and then he stopped thirty meters away from the graves.

The old man, who was standing in front of them, turned toward the boy and drawled, "Come on, Strawberry. Your kin are glad you're here. They won't haunt you."

The boy took a few steps closer, stopped, and then he slowly walked to his grandfather's side. In the fading sunlight, the boy's eyes scanned four ornately decorated stone tombs glowing like sculptures of ice on top of the well-manicured mound.

The old man said softly without looking at the boy, "My great grandfather, your great-great-great grandfather is buried on the far left with his wife. He built our san-ho yuan by hand, by himself in 1875. Brick by brick. If that doesn't make you feel proud, we should dig a hole for you shortly. Next to him are my grandfather and grandmother, your great-great grandfather and grandmother, and next to them are my father and my mother. And next to them is my wife, your grandmother," he said and his voice trailed off. "You probably don't remember her very well."

"Some."

"You should. She doted on you something awful."

The old man knelt down in front of a weathered half-meter-tall shrine that sat in front of the graves. A yellow robed statue of Tu Di Gong, the Earth god, sat inside.

"He's watched over our family for a hundred years," the old man said, and lit incense found inside.

They stood up after they prayed.

The boy pointed to an unmarked grave in a small mound of its own five meters to the right of the larger mound and asked, "What's that grave over there?"

"Let's get some supper," the old man said, and he turned and walked toward the house pretending not to hear the question. The flashing lights again appeared at the edges of his vision. Dammit, he thought, that's the first time it's happened two days in a row.

The tired boy was nodding off in bed soon after supper. He heard footsteps outside. He went to the window and saw his grandfather stride five meters past the courtyard and into the broad moonlit clearing in front of the dirt road.

The old man gazed at the mango trees and full moon and began the graceful movements of *chi gong*. Chi gong focuses on increasing one's "chi" life energy, spiritual enlightenment, and physical flexibility. The grove of mango trees swayed gently in the warm evening breeze as if directed by the old man's movements.

"He looks like a swan," the boy said in disbelief as he stared at his grandfather. "He's changed."

The boy watched the old man for a long time. Curtis picked up his wallet off the dresser and pulled out a small color photo of his parents. He held the photo up in the moonlight and looked at it.

He put the photo away and took off his shirt. The moonlight lit up the scars on his abdomen and chest. He ran his fingers along them.

He retrieved a straight razor that he'd hidden in the top dresser drawer. He flipped the razor open and made a three-inch-long cut on his chest. He watched the blood trickle. He smeared it around, then hid the razor and timidly went back to the window. Shame came upon him as it always did when he cut himself. He couldn't watch his grandfather anymore.

The boy put his shirt on and got in bed. He paged through a book that his grandfather left for him; poetry by the Taiwanese poet Loa Ho. He began reading the first poem the same way he picked at his supper.

Ten minutes later the boy heard people speaking in English from across the courtyard.

"Damn him. He's got a TV!" the boy exclaimed, and he jumped out of bed, went out the door and marched across the courtyard toward his grandfather's door.

A blue light from a TV glowed in the window. The boy glanced at his chest as he stood in the open doorway. He was thankful no blood had seeped through his shirt. His grandfather was sitting in a chair with his back to him watching *To Kill a Mockingbird* on TV.

"No TV, huh," the boy said.

His grandfather turned, smiled mischievously and said, "Not for Strawberries. Read Loa Ho. It may improve your vision. You might earn access to my library."

The boy shrugged with a slight scowl.

The old man said, "Reading can keep your mind in a state of eternal spring. An ignorant man dies the same death every day," and he shooed the boy away.

The boy trudged back to his room and went to bed without looking at Lao Ho's book of poetry.

Delirium seized the old man at the end of *To Kill a Mockingbird*. The unmarked grave in back of the house that the boy asked about loomed before him. He shook and sweat with eyes shut.

3

Hai Lee was ten years old in the spring of 1944. A *Hinomaru*, the Japanese flag, flew over the family san-ho yuan.

The horrors of World War II and their Japanese masters had the Taiwanese by the throat. They'd suffered under Japanese colonization since 1895.

From 1936 until the end of war, the Japanese increased the suffering as they stripped Taiwan of its coal, agriculture and timber for its conflict against China and the Allies and instituted the Kominka movement with the goal of fully Japanizing Taiwanese society.

Many Taiwanese were forced to learn to speak Japanese, wear Japanese clothing and convert to Shintoism. The Colonial Government shrewdly began the Kominka movement to achieve loyalty and cooperation among the locals. Without it, they didn't have the manpower to deplete Taiwan of its natural resources. Young Taiwanese men, some only sixteen, were forced to become soldiers for the Japanese Imperial Army—imprisoned or killed if they refused.

Hai's father liked to say the boy was made of baling wire, salt and kerosene. Like other boys his age, Hai was required to learn Japanese two hours a week, and sometimes beaten if he spoke Taiwanese. Hai was the top Japanese speaker in his class and the biggest screw off. This infuriated his instructor.

Hai's dropping out of elementary school was common among rural children. Fortunately for him, his father not only taught him to read and write, but bought him many books ranging from basic botany to the Opium Wars.

Hai's father also began creating a library in the san-ho yuan. Books were hard to come by during World War II, nearly as difficult during the ensuing decades of Martial Law imposed by self-appointed dictator Chiang-kai Shek and his Kuomintang Party.

But Hai's father was cunning and relentless in his pursuit of books. He combed the black market, made under-the-table deals with librarians, and traded crops for books. The collection slowly grew. Hai's father added to and tended the collection as carefully as he'd later nurture the mangos.

Hai would come to prize his modest collection. During Hai's teen years his father added many volumes to the library; Plato and Aristotle, the *Tao Te Ching*, *The Analects of Confucius*, poetry and more. One of his favorites became a translation of *My First Summer in the*

Sierra written by John Muir in 1911.

In 1944 there were no mango trees on Hai's father's property. The first mango scions didn't come to Taiwan until the 1960s. For decades, the family had made a sufficient living growing and selling wax apples.

In 1938 the Colonial Government burned the entire orchard and ordered the family to grow rice and cabbage, taken to feed Japanese soldiers at the airfield in nearby Gangshan. Four-year-old Hai cried as he stood with his parents watching their orchards burn. The flame's fury. Tree limbs cracking like bones. Wax apples hissing, screeching before exploding.

His father was given a pittance for the rice and cabbage, barely enough to feed his wife and son. Hai worked in the rice and cabbage fields with his mother and father, often twelve hours a day, six days a week.

On a balmy March 1944 dusk a red sun surrendered to boiling yellow clouds. Hai worked a cabbage field near the road. The sound of chains and insults barked by a Japanese soldier startled him. Dust rose on the other side of a rise in the road less than thirty meters away. Three Japanese soldiers and seven prisoners appeared on top of the rise—Taiwanese deserters who'd been forced to join the Japanese Imperial Army. Teenage boys mostly, skeletal, diseased, numbed by weeks of captivity in a place called Bamboo Heaven.

While captive, they'd countless discussions about rumors regarding fates of other deserters. They weren't uttering a word now, how they'd be used for bayonet practice or have wires attached to their genitals and given a "Tokyo phone call," then shot.

Hai'd heard the stories too. All the locals had. Hai recognized a prisoner—a neighbor boy. Hai called out his name but the boy didn't look at him.

"Damn butterheads," Hai yelled at the soldiers as the clink-clank stink-stank passed by. "Their ghosts will follow you forever you bastards."

The soldiers laughed. As they drew away down the road the neighbor boy looked back at Hai with screaming eyes. Then they were gone.

Hai resumed working the row of cabbage. He began to fret the war would drag on and that he too would be forced to join the Japanese Imperial Army. His spirits plummeted further. His hope waned that he and his parents would survive the "Jap Devils" until they were defeated and forced to leave Taiwan.

Hai turned as he heard his father's whistle and soon joined his parents as they walked single file toward the san-ho yuan along the meter-wide dirt berm separating rice fields. The air reeked of Japanese fighter fuel and diesel as it had almost every day since the US declared war on the Empire of the Sun after the attack on Pearl Harbor.

With the Gangshan Airbase nearby, san-ho yuans in the area had been strafed with machine gun fire from American P-51 Mustangs several times in the past few months. Hai's family had been lucky. A neighbor had a dozen fist-sized bullet holes along the back of his house.

Hai's father led the way as they continued toward the san-ho yuan; lean and impassive in a bamboo paddy hat, knee-length black workman's pants and matching button-down jacket made from locally grown hemp.

Hai's mother, Dan-dan Lee, long known as the most

stunning woman in Ciatou, carried a straw basket containing two heads of cabbage. She was dressed in identical yellow clothing and wore a white cotton scarf across her face to shield it from the sun, and more importantly, to conceal her beauty from any passing Japanese officers.

Hai lagged behind, scowling as he tugged on his white hemp shirt with the words "loud mouth" hand written in Japanese.

The father yelled without looking back, "Wear the shirt until your teacher says you can take it off."

Hai growled and spit in disgust at the Hinomaru hanging limp against the sky above their san-ho yuan. He remembered the day two years before when a Japanese patrol of three men with shiny rifles came to put up the flag. He winced as he recalled his parents' bleak expressions—his mother gasping as the flag was raised. And later, his father telling him how a neighbor who protested bitterly was shot dead while a Hinomaru was raised over his san-ho yuan.

When they reached the house, they rinsed mud off their bare feet and legs from a well pump, hung their hats by the front door, and went inside to the ancestral shrine that occupied the small room. Dan-dan took the cabbages into the kitchen and began preparing a meal of rice, cabbage and boiled duck eggs.

Hai assisted his father in tidying up the altar, clearing away incense ash and fallen orchid petals. His father lit a new stick of incense, thick as a cigar and twelve inches long, and placed it in the urn in the center of the altar. He then lit six thin sticks of incense and handed three to the boy. They knelt in front of the altar, held the incense close to their faces and prayed in silence.

Hai's father trembled slightly, prayed for courage for what he was about to do. What he felt compelled to do. Hai prayed for terrible things to happen to his Japanese teacher. Then he thought about the Taiwanese prisoners who were marched past him that afternoon. The neighbor boy's screaming eyes.

Dan-dan was wearing a pink kimono when the pair came into the kitchen to eat. Her husband gave her nervous glances as they ate. Hai took notice and prepared for another lecture concerning proper school behavior.

When he finished eating the man said to his wife, "Bring me Kaoliang, Dan-dan."

She brought him a glass and a bottle of the clear, potent alcohol made from the sorghum plant on nearby Kinmen Island. She slipped out of the kitchen. Hai stood up.

"Sit," said his father.

The boy sat back down. His father took a pack of Paradise cigarettes out of his paddy jacket, lit one, took a long drag, poured a shot of Kaoliang, threw it down followed by another. The man's face softened.

He gazed somberly at Hai and said, "I want to tell you something." He hesitated and said deadpan, "Your mother. Your mother was raped by a Japanese officer eleven years ago. By your real father."

The boy's eyes flew open.

"You're not—?"

"Understand?" He exhaled, took another shot, eyed the boy apologetically.

The boy sat speechless, then whispered, "What's the Jap Devil's name?"

"Death."

"The name?" Hai shouted.

"Your mother will never tell me. She fears I'll go after him and get killed."

"Is he still here?"

"No."

The boy knew he was lying. He thought of his mother. Tears rolled. Then silence.

Mr. Lee said, "You can't say a word about this to anyone. It's our secret. If the soldiers find out you've been asking questions it could be our end. Understand?"

Hai burst out crying. "Papa, then why did you tell me?"

"This crazy war. In case anything happens to me and your mother. You need to know who you are."

The boy jumped up, ran to him, wrapped his arms around his chest and cried and wailed. His father began to sob.

Dan-dan Lee had been sitting in the next room listening. She appeared in the kitchen doorway, standing straight and strong, a gentle smile raining on the pair.

Hai and her husband went to her.

Hai lay awake that night—enraged—afraid.

He thought, if something so horrible could happen to Mother, what will happen next? He vowed to find the officer who raped his mother and kill him to save family honor.

Hai wondered how he could do it. The Officer's Club at the Gangshan Airbase, that's where the bastard will be. Getting drunk. Everyone's heard about the wild things that happen at that place. Wen-hsiung sells cigarettes there. He's twelve, only two years older than me.

Damn. If he can sell there I can, too. But, I can't ask him where the Japs keep the cigarettes. Nobody can know my plan. I'll rig a cigarette tray and swipe the Jap's cigs and sell them back to the devils. I can sneak over to the base at night. I'll find him. Follow him to his barracks. He'll be drunk. I need a knife. A gun.

Hai went to Gangshan Airbase three nights later. He waited for his parents to fall asleep, climbed out his window, then cautiously rode his father's bicycle the three-and-a-half kilometers and hid it among banana trees just outside the base's perimeter.

He felt lucky that he hadn't come upon Japanese patrols. The base was dark. Only a few lights shined in the distance.

Moonlight faintly illuminated the thin runway. It looked okay now, Hai thought. Good. He'd remembered his father telling him that P-51 Mustangs had bombed the runway twice in the past three months. Each time the Japanese worked day and night to repair it. He'd worried that if the Americans bombed the base too much they might move it too far away along with the man who'd raped his mother—his biological father.

Hai took a deep breath and dashed across fifty meters of open ground, and entered a coconut palm grove that ran along the runway's east side. He soon came upon a sign nailed to the trunk of a tree near the grove's edge.

It read: Military Personnel Only Beyond This Point. Violators Will Be Executed.

Hai said, "Hell with that," and continued along stealthily.

Left of the grove, yellow straw roofs of two long, narrow buildings soon came into view. Two larger buildings loomed behind each. Hai darted from tree to tree until he was at the edge of the grove, thirty meters behind the first narrow building.

He smelled cigarette smoke and heard laughter, and quickly fell into a crouch behind one of the thick palms. It got quiet ten minutes later.

He waited another ten minutes, ran to the rear of the first building, and with his back against it moved around the side to the front corner. He peered out. A Japanese soldier guarded the front door holding an Arisaka Type 99 bolt-action rifle against his shoulder.

Hai waited. After twenty minutes the guard walked to the other side of the building. Hai ran out and read the sign above the door: Supply Building 2.

"Yes," Hai whispered, "they must store the cigarettes here or in the hut next door."

He dashed back to the corner of the building and as he crept along its side froze when he heard planes above. Red runway marker lights began to blink. The base came alive. Jeeps revved. Wide doors screeched open from both of the larger buildings. Men poured out. The roar of the incoming planes grew louder.

Hai turned and ran to the palm grove and knelt behind a tree at its edge. He looked at the sky. The first Zero approached from the south, descended, and landed followed by five more. Jeeps raced to each plane. He watched the first pilot climb out of his plane and get into a Jeep.

Hai's eyes followed the Jeep to the north of the runway, veer right and disappear behind the northeast corner of the coconut palm grove.

He raced 150 meters to the northern edge of the palm grove, crawled through meter-high grass until he heard shouting and laughter and music. Hai looked up.

There it was, fifty meters away—the Officer's Club. The boy smiled, pleased with his night's work. But, how am I going to steal the cigs, he thought? Guards are probably posted at the supply huts every night. What else can I hawk to the officers? I've got to get inside the Officer's Club. The bastard who raped Mother is probably in there right now!

Hai made his way home and crawled into bed without waking his parents. It was two a.m.

Hai returned to Gangshan Airbase three nights later. Again, he hid his father's bicycle in the banana trees and made his way north through the coconut palm grove. He stopped in the tall grass north of the grove as he had before. The club boiled. Officers came and went.

Hai crept counterclockwise and crouched in a cluster of papaya trees directly behind the Officer's Club's back door, where a youthful Japanese soldier washed dishes in a tub.

Hai took a deep breath, closed his eyes and prayed to the goddess Kuanyin, "Oh, blessed Kuanyin, help me say the right things to this Jap dog scum. This ugly monkey," and he stood up and walked toward the soldier, who didn't notice him until he was five meters away.

"What the hell are you doing here, chink?" The soldier hissed and splashed dishwater at the boy.

"I heard you need some help," Hai spoke in Japanese.

"Huh? I could plug you, you know."

"Yeah."

"A tough little runt, huh?" The soldier laughed.

Hai shrugged. "I bet you're a samurai," he said, trying

to flatter the soldier.

"Of course," the soldier said with pluck and stuck his nose in the air. "I was doing sword tricks in the womb. I'll cut your fingers and ears off fast as lightning." The soldier splashed more water toward Hai and yelled, "Blow."

"I'll bus tables for you two nights a week. Whatever nights you're working. After ten. For a meal each night."

"Beat it."

Hai feigned a pout and said, "I heard another local kid sells cigarettes here."

"He got fired."

Good, thought Hai. There's no chance word can get to my parents I'm here. "Why'd he get fired?"

"For being a lousy thieving chink," the soldier said, and went back to work.

Hai stayed put. The soldier looked up after he scrubbed and rinsed several plates, wiped his hands on his apron, walked over and picked up an Arisaka rifle that leaned against the building behind him. His hands trembled as he pointed it at Hai.

Hai stood still. "You've never shot anybody."

The soldier moved closer until he was a few meters in front of Hai. He pointed the rifle at the ground. "Get lost. Go on."

Hai turned and walked away.

The soldier called out, "I scrape plates Tuesdays and Thursdays." Hai stopped and turned around. "I'll talk to my sergeant. Come back Thursday."

"Thank you," said Hai, and he turned and disappeared into the grass.

"Crazy little chink," the soldier shook his head and

laughed. He liked him.

Thursday night. 9:45 p.m. On his way to the Officer's Club Hai was confident he could speak Japanese well enough to deal with the officers and understand their conversations.

He began bussing tables shortly after he arrived. Officers and pilots crowded around twenty tables drinking sake and Kaoliang in a haze of cigarette smoke. Most of them were tanked, bragging and name calling and shouting *kanpai* (bottoms up).

A boogie-woogie tune sung by Misora Hibari poured from speakers behind a long bar. There was a piano, several card and dice tables, a Hinomaru on the wall.

"Our own private Shina pig," an officer yelled and pointed at Hai.

Many officers rubbed their knuckles across the top of the boy's head as he passed by.

A chubby captain yelled, "Wooly coolie."

Hai was dead tired after two hours of carrying his bamboo tray of dirty dishes and glasses to the dishwasher.

"Lots of officers at this base, huh?" Hai said to the soldier dishwasher.

"You a spy?"

"Yeah."

"Maybe a hundred. Maybe a thousand. All psychotic. At one we knock off. Your dinner will be waiting in the kitchen. Ask the cook."

On his way home Hai thought about how he could find out which officers had been stationed at the base for ten years or more. These would be the suspects in the rape of his mother—his real father.

4

Three days had passed since Curtis's arrival at his grand-father's san-ho yuan.

As they ate lunch on the porch after another morning's work, the old man was relieved that he hadn't had a delirium episode since the night his grandson came. But, he worried about the boy witnessing an episode and what lies he should tell him.

The old man looked up from his plate of fish and rice. "Reading Lao Ho? The book I left on your nightstand."

"Yeah."

"Summarize his first poem."

The boy blushed.

"Better read up," the old man said sternly, and then he smiled. "The library's waiting for you. Next week I'm going to give you Hemmingway's Old Man and the Sea.

And something new each following week."

The boy nodded with little enthusiasm.

A black Mercedes with mirrored windows pulled up to the san-ho yuan.

"Kuomintang," snarled the old man.

"How do you know?"

"Stench makes my nose run," he said with eyes fixed on the car.

A young man wearing a sharkskin suit, machete tie, got out of the Benz. He walked stiff-legged up to the porch with a slippery smile. His gold Rolex sparkled in the sun.

The old man stood up, inflated his chest. He looked the stranger over and said, "'A covetous man's ever in want.'"

"Pardon?"

"Horace."

"Who?"

"A Greek. You should know him. He warned about your kind. Filthy thieves. The corrupt."

The man's slippery smile slipped further. "I'm sorry, I don't—"

"Awful shrill voice, son. Briefs too tight?"

"What? A joke, huh? Funny."

The young man tried to smile through a frown, pulled a red envelope called a *hung-bao* out of his coat pocket, held it delicately in front of him with both hands and was about to step onto the porch when the old man snapped, "I just washed this damn porch."

The man stopped a few meters from the porch. The sun began to carve into him.

Tension muted the boy. He studied his grandfather,

sat up, gripped the armrests tight.

"I'm an official of the Kuomintang Party. I'm authorized to give you this—"

"Bribe," shot the old man.

"Divine incentive," the young official continued. "For the upcoming election."

The old man roared in mocking laughter.

He turned toward Curtis and asked, "What they call that crap the Americans use a lot now? That gibberish?"

"Politically correct."

"That's it," he said, and turned back toward the young official and blasted, "a perversion of the language. Phony as your get up."

Sweat rolled down the KMT official's face. He continued to hold the hung-bao out with both hands.

"Fly-catcher, how much you got in there?"

"Five hundred NT." Fifteen American dollars.

The old man thrust his hands to his cheeks, feigned excitement.

"Your family has greatly benefited for many years from Chiang-kai Shek's benevolence and opportunities he's allotted Taiwanese farmers," the KMT official said.

"I suppose."

The young man smiled and inched closer without stepping on the porch.

The old man drawled, "Ever witness a murder?"

"God no!"

"Ever seen a corpse? Oozing like the end of the world. Shimmering with black flies, maggots?"

"Please, mister. I didn't mean—"

"Chiang-kai Shek—a megalomaniac on a good day. A killer when he had a bad day. Bastard had lots of bad bad days. And idiots like you still worship the son of a bitch."

The KMT official worked hard to prop up a smile. "That was a long time ago."

The old man turned toward Curtis, shot the boy a prosecuting look and said out of the corner of his mouth, "Some kid told me the exact same thing the other day."

Curtis felt embarrassed as he remembered he gave his grandfather the same reply when he spoke of the Japanese atrocities during World War II.

The old man turned back to the young official. "Show us your profile."

"I uh, don't understand."

"Who does your portrait? A police sketch artist?"

The KMT official tried to recall a lesson from his training called "dealing with spirited citizens."

"You should go now," said the old man.

The official walked halfway out of the courtyard and stopped, turned around, scratched his head and yelled, "Are you somebody famous?"

"I'm somebody with a shotgun."

The man stood there for a while with a puzzled expression on his face, and then he turned and quick-stepped to the Benz.

The old man plopped down in his chair. "I need a shot of Kaoliang."

The boy went to the kitchen and returned with a bottle of Tunnel 88 and a glass.

The boy sat down. "You have a shotgun?"

"Nope. You are aware that a law exists prohibiting private citizens from owning firearms."

"Of course, but I thought, oh, forget it. This happened before? The KMT."

"Every election. I think my reply to the bribe is getting better," he said proudly.

"You enjoyed it?"

"Relished it. Think I was hard on that kid?"

"Yes."

"I would've been imprisoned, maybe killed if I'd said those things during Chiang-kai Shek's dictatorship."

"I've studied about the 'White Terror.'"

The old man frowned. "It was real, kid. Tell me you know when Martial Law ended."

"1987."

"'The devil hath power to assume a pleasing shape.'"

The boy shrugged with a quizzical look.

"Shakespeare," said the old man. "That'll be a good one for you. I'll put it in your room." He took a shot of Kaoliang and stood up. "Change your 'hoodlum' shirt."

"I don't have to wear it anymore?"

"Wear it here. We're going out."

"Oh, okay," said the boy, realizing his grandfather didn't want him seen wearing the shirt in public because the old man would lose face.

The boy dragged across the courtyard toward his room not caring where they were headed. It beat toiling in the sun and mango orchard.

They left on the old man's muddy motorcycle. After five kilometers they turned onto a straight narrow road. At its end, 400 meters away, sat Golden Lotus Temple. It was monolithic, jewel-like. Vast rice and lettuce fields spread out behind it.

The old man slowed down to gaze at wide sunflower fields that stretched along both sides of the road to the small parking lot.

Their radiance and the temple sparkling in the distance couldn't penetrate the boy.

The smiling old man continued to admire the sunflowers, the temple in the distance. He was pleased with himself that this scene always took his breath away.

Cumulus clouds fumed on the horizon, outlined in pink in the sun. They seemed to elevate the temple above the ground, transforming it into a gateway between man and gods—life and death.

The old man looked back, noticed the boy's disinterest. He slowed down to fifteen kph, 200 meters from the entrance.

The boy purposely yawned in the old man's ear, unimpressed with the temple's brilliant yellow roof, its width adorned with statues of dragons, winged horses, a parade of deities. The old man slowed further.

"The sun's cooking me," the boy griped.

The old man turned the motorcycle around, drove back to the end of the road, stopped. "Get the hell off and walk."

"Sorry."

"Off."

The boy obeyed.

The old man continued toward the temple, stopped outside the temple gate at a betel nut stand near several food vendors.

A betel nut girl appeared in the glass booth's door. She was nineteen, hot as the surface of Mercury, wearing a silver mini-dress covered with red stars. A red-feather boa around her neck. Her attire typical for a betel nut girl. The old man got off his motorcycle and walked up to the girl.

"Hello, Mr. Lee," she said politely.

"Hey, Lightning. New ladybug boots?"

"Ladybug," she laughed coyly, liking the way he teased her. "They're Happy Go boots. Like the astronauts wear. I saw these crazy Brazilian dancers wearing them when they were here on New Year's Eve."

"Nice," said the old man, but he didn't mean it. "How've you been, space girl?"

"Out of my mind."

"You mean you drive guys out of their minds."

"My sister stripped for a magazine."

Lightning's boss, shady as the dark side of the moon, stuck his head out of the booth, sneered, then ducked back inside.

The old man jerked his head toward the booth, and said to the girl, "Quit this racket before you get your wings cut off."

Lightning chuckled uneasily. "Blue Boy's harmless."

"Sure. The punk who ran this aquarium before him?"

Lightning looked down, pitched her shoulders around uncomfortably. "Taipei Prison," she mumbled. "You know that," she meowed, her feelings hurt.

"Sorry. My evil tiger's on the prowl."

He glanced at the boy up the road, who was 200 meters away, slowly making his way toward the temple.

The old man turned grim, leveled his eyes at Lightning. "It's relentless," he said.

"Huh? What is?"

"The past."

"Mr. Lee are you—?"

"It keeps coming and coming."

Lightning looked passed him at the boy up the road.

"What's wrong Mr. Lee?"

"How's your mother?"

The girl stole glances at the boy as she said, "So so. Not so good sometimes."

"Your sister stripped for cash, huh. Jealous? You better not be."

He torched a cig, turned and gave the boy a longer look this time. Curtis was 150 meters away, zigzagging and kicking stones as he stared at the ground.

"Watched you drive up," Lightning said, "then turn back and drop that boy. What for?"

"My grandson." The old man blew a smoke ring. "The past's hammerin' the kid."

She wanted to ask if the past was hammering the old man, but remembered how her mother often tells her it's rude and not ladylike to be direct. Instead, she said politely, "Taking him to pray."

"Be sweet to him, huh."

"What's his name?"

"Right now? Son of a bitch. His given name's Li Wei."

Lightning laughed.

"He's hard up," said the old man with a playful wink. "Looking for a way out. Might want to run off with a betel nut beauty."

The girl laughed harder. Blue Boy, her boss, zoomed out from behind the betel nut stand on a scooter and headed east of the temple.

The old man watched him drive away. "Know what would make me happy?" he said.

She jokingly fluttered her eyebrows, cupped her small breasts.

"Not that. If I were to come here one day and you'd be gone. Enrolled full-time in a university."

"I can't. You know I have to work to help my—"

"'Learn as though you would never be able to master it.'"

Lightning smiled humbly and completed the verse by Confucius, "'And hold it as though you would be in fear of losing it.'"

"See? You should be running this country."

Her cheeks reddened. "Hey, here comes your grandson."

The pair turned as the boy walked up.

Lightning took a few steps forward and said, "Hi Li Wei. Like your hairstyle. It's cute."

The boy blushed, hot as the surface of Mercury. "Hi," he said with a little smile. "It's Curtis."

The old man grinned. "Two boxes today, Lightning," he said and paid her.

Lightning went inside, returned and handed him two cigarette-box-size packages of betel nuts. The old man and boy said goodbye to Lightning, climbed on the motorcycle and drove through the arched gate, parked in a row of ten scooters at the foot of the steep temple steps.

"Don't tell these rascals your foreigner name," warned the old man.

The boy shrugged unconcerned, and as the pair climbed the steps he asked, "Why she called Lightning?"

"170 IQ."

"Wow."

"Her sister's name is Elephant."

"Elephant?"

"Weighs about a hundred kilos."

"No," cackled the boy.

"Photographic memory. IQ in the clouds."

As they entered the cavernous temple Curtis wondered if Elephant was beautiful like her sister.

The temple was empty of pilgrims. Incense smoke drifted from a brass dragon urn inside the door. Murals depicting heroics of gods and goddesses covered the walls and the forty-meter-high ceiling. Life-sized statues of Kuanyin, Buddha, and six folk deities dressed in bright robes stood in elaborate compartments spanning the rear wall.

Golden Lotus Temple's a polytheistic folk shrine. In Taiwan it's common to worship Taoist, Buddhist, and folk deities in such places.

Altars in front of the gods were covered with vases of orchids, offerings of fruit, snacks, candy, and soda.

The old man went to a counter and bought ghost money and incense. Ghost money is used as an offering to gods and deceased ancestors.

He lit the incense and knelt in front of Kuanyin, the same deity glorifying his san-ho yuan's altar. The boy knelt next to him. The old man handed three sticks to the boy and prayed for guidance on how to help his grandson.

The boy prayed for his parents. Five minutes passed. The old man got up and knelt in front of Luxing, god for students. The boy didn't pray for himself. He didn't think he was worth it.

The old man rose. The boy lagged behind. They stuck their incense in the sandy bottom of the dragon urn by the entrance, descended the steps and walked to a ten-meter-high chimney that sat apart on the right side of the temple. It was painted with mythic scenes.

The old man opened the small door at the chimney's base. He gave half the ghost money to the boy. They folded several pieces at a time and tossed them into the fire until all the money was gone.

They went back upstairs to the temple's social room, separated by a wall from the prayer area. Men gambled and drank around rattan tables. A TV flashed a game show next to a Karaoke station where a bargirl in hot pants and bikini top murdered *Tie a Yellow Ribbon Round the Ole Oak Tree.*

The old man strode to a table, surveyed the faces of his aged pals, bottles of Taiwan Beer and Kaoliang. A pile of one-hundred-dollar NT notes (each worth three US dollars).

The old man's best friend, Professor Kung, waved and smiled at him and the boy. Kung was a recently retired "professor emeritus" from the renowned National Taiwan University where he taught Chinese literature. He was beefy, handsome, with slicked back gray hair.

"Who's the strawberry, Hai?" yelled a dairy farmer above the commotion.

"My grandson, Li Wei."

"Curtis," the boy blurted meekly.

"Oooh, well," a papaya grower yelped.

A fat banana grower yawped, "Sounds like a rice queen."

Everyone laughed except Professor Kung, who petulantly tugged on the sleeve of his yellow polo shirt and adjusted his glasses.

"Told you so," the old man said to the boy out of the

corner of his mouth. Curtis took a step back.

The temple spirit medium's eyes danced over his cards. "Suckers," he laughed and flipped two hundred NT into the pot. Professor Kung folded.

The dairy farmer matched the raise along with the other players and scoffed, "Shave his head, Hai? You do that? He looks so so cool. A little notorious."

"A strawberry milkshake," the papaya grower exclaimed, and sang in a high pitched key, "strawberries grow to be such sweet things."

More laughter.

"Strawberry pie. Strawberry Jell-O."

The professor shook his head in disapproval.

"Shut up," growled a retired policeman.

"Strawberry jam."

"Hey, Milkshake," a janitor leaning on his broom shouted. "Good name for him. Milkshake. I think so."

A thirty-year-old stockbroker from Taipei, visiting his new father-in-law the papaya grower, waved a hand at the boy and railed, "The extortionist, huh. A hundred more," and threw in three hundred. His eyes zeroed on Hai's. "He ain't locked up?"

The old man stood coolly as the men matched the raise.

"Shut up," bawled Professor Kung. His eyes menacingly scanned the others.

"Yeah," said the policeman.

"Oh yeah," sang the stockbroker. "Heard the sad tale yesterday about the poor schoolgirl. Curtis tries to fleece any of my family and I'll press charges."

Hai Lee stared deadpan at the stockbroker then looked away. He lit a cigarette.

The papaya grower leaned toward his new son-in-law

the stockbroker, whispered so no one could hear, "Hai Lee makes a bad enemy."

"Sit in, Hai," Professor Kung said. "You were up last month."

The old man shrugged, walked to a nearby counter, grabbed a bottle of beer, gulped half of it.

The dairy farmer leaned in from the stockbroker's other side and whispered, "Hai survived the Jap occupation. The White Terror. He's done things too terrible for words. He saved someone's life when he was a kid. He's known as the Boy Hero of Ciatou." He nudged the stockbroker, who ran eyes north and south over Hai. "Seventy-two," the dairy farmer continued with awe, "still a very dangerous man."

The stockbroker yawned as if bored. He was too arrogant to comprehend the weight of the dairy farmer's words.

The old man finished his beer, shot the stockbroker a final stare, and without looking at anyone said softly, "Business," and motioned to the spirit medium, who got up and followed him and Curtis into a side altar inside the prayer area.

The old man handed the spirit medium a jade pendant of Kuanyin on a silver chain. The spirit medium, dressed in a traditional red and yellow vest over his tattooed torso, waved a fan of anointed feathers and passed the pendant three times over incense smoke pouring from the small urn on the altar. The old man and Curtis looked on as he danced around praying, taking swigs from a bottle of Kaoliang.

The spirit medium stopped and draped the necklace around the boy's neck. "Wear it always," he said.

"Kuanyin'll show you mercy."

"Thanks," the boy said, and he turned and smiled timidly at his grandfather.

Professor Kung was waiting for Hai Lee and the boy when they walked out to the temple steps. He introduced himself to Curtis, patted his friend on the shoulder and offered him a few words of consolation and support before the pair said goodbye and descended the steps.

The old man wouldn't have shown any hint of embarrassment or lost his cool no matter what insults or jabs the stockbroker came up with. Losing one's composure or temper in public in Taiwanese culture is taboo and a serious loss of face.

As they straddled the motorcycle, the old man said, "Auntie said you liked MacDonald's."

The boy smiled as they pulled out of the parking lot.

5

The next morning the old man woke up at 5:30 and got dressed. Again, the flashing lights appeared at the edges of his vision.

He ignored them, poked his head in Curtis's room and said, "Harvest today."

The boy rolled over, sat up in bed, and wheezed, "You said next month."

"Get dressed, kid. Big day. The mothers of all the goddesses."

"What's that?"

The old man leaned against the door frame, grinned. "My Irwin mangos. Hurry. Breakfast is waiting."

After breakfast the boy followed his grandfather into the home's family shrine, as he'd done every day, where he again mimicked the old man's every move and gesture. The old man stood up after he prayed. He wobbled and had to put his hands on the altar to keep from falling.

"What's wrong?" cried Curtis, and he jumped up.

"I can't see straight. Everything's blurry. Dammit to hell." He rubbed his eyes for several seconds, stopped and blinked four or five times. "There, it's okay now."

The boy gave him a worried look as he watched him walk onto the porch, grab his bamboo hat off the wall, and barrel out into the courtyard. The boy followed.

An old blue coaster bicycle was propped up against the house.

The old man jumped on the bicycle and yelled, "Strawberry Jell-O!" and he flew out of the courtyard, across the dirt drive, and into the mango orchard.

The boy ran after his grandfather as fast as he could and yelled as he entered the orchard, "Where's my bike?"

"Come on, Milkshake," the old man turned his head and shouted with the glee of a child.

The boy chased after his grandfather, who was fifty meters ahead and pulling further away each second, then he abruptly turned right on the rickety old bike, and disappeared into the mangos.

The boy laughed, and continued to run after the wily rascal until his lungs blew out. He turned right where he saw his grandfather disappear, and heard women talking.

He ran down a row following the cooing sounds, and after several minutes he came upon the old man, who was standing in the shade near two lean women, watching them as they separated red mangos into two flat plastic bins that were sitting on top of a meter-high stack of their empty brothers. The panting, sweaty boy stopped in front of his grandfather.

"Your eyes okay?" said Curtis.

The old man ignored the question. "Get lost?" he bawled lightheartedly.

The boy blushed.

The two women, who were clad in knee-high rubber boots, cotton pants and shirts, and bamboo hats with scarves wrapped around their faces, giggled while they kept working.

One of the women looked up at the boy and noticed his "hoodlum" shirt.

"Boy Hero, is this your grandson?" she asked.

The old man winced when he heard the words "Boy Hero," as if he'd been struck with a bamboo stick.

Curtis saw his grandfather's face change, and he thought that he looked almost afraid.

"Uh-huh," the old man said, concealing his disappointment with the woman. He'd told the pickers moments before the boy appeared not to refer to him as Boy Hero as they usually did, but to call him Mr. Lee in front of his grandson.

The woman's companion, the taller of the two, cupped her hand over her mouth and shouted into the trees, "We've got a convict here!" and squealed with laughter.

From somewhere up in the trees a female voice shouted, "Is he cute?"

"He's a real pretty boy," she yelled back and everyone laughed.

Curtis became self-conscious, ashamed, as he often felt when people complimented his looks. He envisioned the horror of the ladies if they saw his scars.

The old man picked one of the hand-sized mangos

out of a bin, held it up to his face and smelled it; then he reached out and held it under the boy's nose, and said tenderly, "The sweetest smell in the world."

He outstretched his arms, looked at the surrounding ten-meter-tall trees, and exclaimed, "These boy, are my Irwin mango trees. My gold mine. I've got fifty producing trees that run to the property line next to that rice field over yonder."

The boy looked through the rows of Irwin trees and into the sun-drenched rice field, the meter-high stalks swaying in the warm breeze.

The old man looked at the bin on his left and said, "These pick of the litter go to Japan, where they can sell for as much as thirty US dollars a piece."

He held the pristine mango out in front of the boy, slowly turned it, and said, "This is the only way the Japs will take them—without as much as a mark the size of a mosquito's ass on it."

"Thirty US a piece?" said the boy, and raised his eyebrows. "Why they called 'Irwin'?"

The old man smiled broadly, pleased with the boy's interest, and orated with the pomp of an exasperating statesman, "F.D. Irwin was a mango grower from Miami, Florida. In 1939 he cross-pollinated a Haden mango variety with a Lippens, and the Irwin was born, first bearing fruit in 1945. In the early 1960s, the first Irwin seedlings arrived in Taiwan, planted in Tainan's Yuching Township. A grower from Tainan County, a friend of your great grandfather, gave the seedlings to him over fifty years ago. And now look at them."

The boy was impressed by the old man's knowledge.

"You know the whole history," he said.

"Damn right, I do," quipped the old man.

He stood silently for a long moment, the proud look on his face turned to melancholy, his shoulders slumped, and he looked off into the mangos.

He turned his head quickly, stared hard at the boy, and asked, "Why do you think the Irwin mango was brought to Taiwan, schoolboy?"

The boy fidgeted, shuffled his feet, and squint his eyes waiting for the storm to hit.

"I don't know," he said softly without looking at his grandfather.

"Because we Taiwanese were too damn poor—poor as poor can be. We needed help. Hell, a man that ate rice and sweet potatoes every night was considered a rich man. Most of us only ate sweet potato leaves, what they fed pigs."

"I didn't—"

The old man cut him off and said, "Know your history boy. Be proud of it, and what we've become. It'll puff out your chest."

The old man put the mango back into the bin, reached into the other bin, plucked out a slightly blemished mango, deftly cut four sections away from the large center seed with a pocket knife, and handed one of them to the boy.

The boy cupped the piece in both hands, put it against his lips, quickly ate the fruit away from the skin, smiled, and exclaimed, "Wow!"

The old man grinned and said, "Now you're learning," and he discarded the mango seed into a nearby bucket and handed each woman a section.

"The blemished ones taste just as delicious as their

fair-haired sisters. I sell them domestically for less than a song."

The old man devoured the remaining mango section, looked at the boy sternly and said, "I'm counting on you today. Remember, handle these beauties as gently as you would a newborn. Follow the ladies. They'll hold your hand and walk you through it."

"Okay," said the boy.

The old man gave the boy another hard stare and said, "I'm going to tend to the Chin-huang mangos. I've been watching your eyes looking down toward the road. You've designs to rabbit to Kaohsiung City. I don't know what's dirtier down there, the air or the people. I'll find you if you run off. Stake you to an ant hill or give you the Cool Hand Luke treatment."

"The what?"

"It's a film. Ol' Luke's in prison like you. He got the rabbit in him. Took off. They caught him. Warden made him dig a grave in the yard. When he finished they made him fill it in and dig it again. And again and again. Finally, Luke drops in the grave from exhaustion."

"Dies?"

"No."

The boy shrugged. "Too bad."

The old man shook his head in displeasure, hopped on his bicycle and disappeared down a row.

Curtis worked all morning with the women, who watched him keenly, and instructed him how to separate the choicest mangos for export to Japan.

The old man returned throughout the morning to check on the boy's progress, sitting under the shade of a mango tree admiring the stacked bins full of Irwins proud as a new father of quintuplet boys.

After lunch the old man walked up to the boy and said, "Get your straw butt up in the tree with Miss Lily over there. And don't go falling down and breaking your ass. I hate going to the damn hospital."

The old man followed behind the boy as he walked over to the mango tree, climbed a step ladder leaning against its trunk, and cautiously climbed into the tree.

"Holy smokers!" bawled the old man. "You'd think you're walking a tightrope strung across Taroko Gorge by the way you pussyfooted that one."

Everyone laughed.

The old man walked directly under the tree and called out, "You stay right on Miss Lily's hip, boy. Don't get any foolish ideas that you know what the hell you're doing. You only pick a mango after Miss Lily tells you which ones are ready."

"Okay," the boy shouted.

"You mind this old bull, or I'll come up there after you, and don't think I can't. Hell, I can still jump around in the mangos like a damn monkey if I'm in the mood."

The women cackled.

By sundown, the boy and the four women had picked and packed ripe mangos from ten of the fifty trees.

A local exporter who the old man had been working with for years showed up at six with a truck and a bundle of crisp, thousand-dollar NT notes. He handed the cash to the smiling old man, loaded up quickly, and drove off.

The old man and the boy stood in the wide, grass covered path at the edge of the property that separated the Irwin mango trees from the adjacent rice field.

The sun waned. The sky a brilliant red-orange. As the women began to ride away on their bicycles the old man called out after them. They stopped in unison, turned around, and saw the old man holding up sacks of mangos.

"Please take some home," he called out.

The women rode up, and one by one, the old man deposited a sack of a half-dozen choice Irwin mangos into the baskets hanging in front of their handlebars.

"Thank you," they cooed softly, giggled, and rode away.

The old man looked at the women affectionately as they disappeared down the dusky orchard row.

"Fine, fine people," he said, and placed his hands on his hips. "Every one of them on the far side of fifty. Hell, any one of them is worth three men in the field." Then he gazed at the boy and said, "I hope you know that you just had the privilege of working with children of the soil."

"I know that," said the boy.

The old man strode to the narrow concrete irrigation channel that ran along the property line in front of the rice field. He propped one foot up on top of the channel, folded his arms across his chest, and looked in admiration across the rice field toward the sunset.

The boy followed, stood near his grandfather, and clumsily propped his foot on top of the irrigation channel. The old man reached into his shirt pocket, grabbed a cigarette, popped into his mouth and lit it.

The old man fixed his eyes on the swaying rice field,

and said without looking at the boy, "If you meditate on a rice field like this one long enough, it'll teach you something you can't express in words. It's a feeling that'll creep into your bones, make you a little better."

"And the mango trees?" asked the boy.

The old man took a long drag off his cigarette, exhaled, looked at the boy and said, "Them, too. Nature's perfect. Man, at his absolute best, a bumbling fool."

The old man turned his gaze back toward the sunset, and with a contented look upon his face, smiled and said, "John Muir wrote, 'Our flesh-and-bone tabernacle seems transparent as glass as to the beauty about us, as if truly an inseparable part of it, thrilling with the air and trees, streams and rocks, in the waves of the sun, a part of all nature, neither old nor young, sick nor well, but immortal.'"

The boy grinned, relaxed his aching shoulders, and took a long slow breath, as if he were trying to inhale his grandfather's words.

"What was he writing about?"

"Mountains in California. The Sierra. From one of my favorite books, My First Summer in the Sierra."

"Ever been there?"

"In my dreams, since I was your age. My father took me and my mother to Snow Mountain near Taichung several times. After that I understood what Muir was trying to express. Ever been to the mountains?"

"Never."

"We should go one day. For a week at least. Up there you can become one with Earth. One with the wild land."

The boy took a few steps closer to his grandfather, and

surveyed the rice field and darkening, red horizon.

Without taking his eyes off the sunset the old man said, "Let's talk about your scars."

This surprised Curtis. He unconsciously ran his hands over his abdomen and chest.

"Not those," said the old man as he kept watching the horizon, "your other scars."

The boy tensed up. Thoughts collided. He remained silent for a long while, and then he said, "My parents, I can't see them . . . only in a photo I have. But I see the girl I extorted money from every day."

"A Greek said, 'through pain to wisdom we find our way.'" The old man hesitated, and then he added, "What a bunch of manure."

The boy eyed him quizzically.

"I've got a scar," the old man said, "seven kilometers long. From here to Gangshan Airbase and back."

The boy waited for the old man to elaborate. They stood in silence for another long moment.

"You've deserved a better grandfather," the old man finally said, and tossed his cig on the ground. "I'm glad you're here."

Curtis smiled slightly and took a deep breath.

The old man said roughly, "Why the hell do you cut yourself, anyway?"

"Diversion."

"Diversion?" the old man scoffed. "Eating an ice cream cone is a diversion. You've got fresh cuts, don't you?"

The boy's silence gave the answer.

"Why."

"I guess I deserve—I deserve to be ugly."

The old man reached to the sky in frustration. He

quickly calmed himself and said, "In every man lives two tigers. One good. One evil. They fight from the day you're born until the day you die."

"Fight for what?"

"Control of your mind. The evil tiger wants you to feel afraid and ashamed. Worthless. Coaxes you to do bad things."

"Which one wins?"

"The one you feed."

Out of respect the boy waited a minute before he said, "I still deserve to be ugly."

"Like hell you do," brayed the old man, and he turned and faced the boy, grabbed him by his shoulders, drew him close and said, "It's making me crazy. Stop that stuff." Then the old man quickly turned back toward the sunset and sparked a cig. "I need you," he said softly.

Those words caused a small breath of serenity to rise up through the boy. His mind wandered to something he'd been nervously contemplating since lunch—the possible consequences he might suffer if he asked his grandfather a question that had been burning in his mind all day.

The pair stood silently until the sun was nearly asleep.

Curtis remembered the pained look on his grandfather's face from that morning, and he asked weakly, "What did she mean when she called you, 'Boy Hero'? Is it connected to the unmarked grave in back?"

The old man ignored the question, popped a betel nut into his mouth and said, "You ride that foul contraption up to the house and get cleaned up for supper. I want to walk."

The boy hopped on the bike and rode through the

orchard toward the house. Thoughts of his grandfather, the "Boy Hero," whatever that meant, flashed in his mind.

"The unmarked grave?" whispered the boy. "And what's wrong with his eyes? He almost keeled over in the shrine room this morning."

The boy couldn't fall asleep that night. After an hour of thrashing around he sat on the end of his bed. He began to sweat. Panic bloomed. Images of his parents and the girl he'd extorted money from flickered. He whimpered and stripped off his shirt.

He went to the dresser, took out the straight razor he'd hidden there, opened it and slowly ran the blade back and forth across his abdomen without breaking the skin. He threw the razor against the wall, dove in bed and began to cry. He cried for ten minutes, until his face and eyes and ears hurt terribly.

Then he remembered his grandfather's words earlier that evening in the mango orchard, "I need you."

No one had ever said that to him before. The words relaxed his mind. The tears stopped. He got up, wrapped the razor in a 7-Eleven bag and threw it in the trash.

That night, a short while later, and the following five nights, the boy sat watching quietly out the bedroom window as his grandfather practiced chi gong.

On the seventh night he stood and tried to follow the old man's movements.

"Why don't you come out here?" said the old man, and he turned his head toward the window.

"How did you know?" asked the boy.

"Come on!"

The boy walked outside and stood next to his grandfather as he continued with his graceful movements.

"Take off your sandals," said the old man.

The boy complied.

"Now you're connected to Earth. Feel it. Feel Earth.
Let its power flow into you, through you. Breathe."

The boy let out a gasp.

"Slowly," the old man growled playfully. "Be here.
Here. Feel each breath. Drop below. Let your mind drop
below the rough water. There is no time down here.
Watch me."

The boy began to awkwardly follow his grandfather's
slow rhythmic movements.

"That's it."

"I know my chi's weak."

"Knowing that has already propelled you further on
your life journey. Through dutiful practice you can find
your true spirit."

The pair continued for another thirty minutes before
going to bed.

The old man couldn't sleep. He sat up on the edge of
his bed. Insomnia ebbed to delirium.

"Tanaka," he cried out. "You you . . ."

The delirium lasted an hour, the longest bout he
could remember.

During the third week of Curtis's incarceration, the
old man woke up at 5:15 on Wednesday morning,
walked to the boy's room to wake him, and stood in
the doorway.

Curtis was sitting on the bed flipping through a *Playboy*. One of the bullies at school who'd forced him to

extort money from the girl gave it to him. When he saw his grandfather, blood surged in his face. He shoved the magazine under his pillow.

The old man entered the room, sat down on the bed and said, "All the pages stuck together?"

The boy looked down in shame.

"This a new 'diversion', or you still cutting? What do you think that Playboy bunny would say if she saw your little blunt?"

The boy frowned and said, "What made you so damn mean?"

The remark caught the old man off guard. He felt like an ass. He rubbed his hands across his shaved head and exhaled.

"Since your dear grandmother passed away nearly five years ago I've become even more ornery than before," he said softly. "She'd find that impossible to believe."

"I wouldn't." A faint smile appeared on the boy's face.

A faraway look appeared in the old man's eyes.

"And other things too, made me the son of a bitch you see here," he muttered, his voice trailing off. He stood up and said, "Breakfast is waiting."

6

Later that week, on Sunday, the old man and Curtis bought two bags of groceries and drove to the betel but girl Lightning's house. Lightning lived with her sister and mother above a Ciatou drug store.

The old man wore a white shirt, tie, and pressed gray slacks. He always dressed up when he visited Lightning's home.

As they each carried a bag up the rundown concrete steps to the third floor, Curtis asked, "Who lives here?"

The old man made the sound of thunder and lightning.

"Her?" the boy said with surprise. "Lightning? The betel nut girl at the temple?"

"Try not to salivate."

Lightning answered the door in sweatpants and a baggy T-shirt. She barely resembled the sultry betel nut girl in the silver dress with red stars, the boy thought.

"Hello, Mr. Lee," Lightning exclaimed. "Please come inside."

The pair entered the small apartment and set the groceries on the dining room table.

Curtis surveyed the clean, modestly furnished space. Several crucifixes hung on the walls along with paintings of Jesus and the Blessed Virgin Mary. His eyes held on an old black-and-white photograph on a nearby wall depicting a fierce-looking male aborigine flanked by companions toting spears and long knives.

Lightning's mother, Mrs. Ari, sat on a red sofa in the center of the living room. She was forty-two, elegant, right out of a 1960s fashion magazine.

"We're always very honored by your visits, Mr. Lee," she said and primped her bouffant hair-do, smoothed out her pristine turquoise print dress. "Please sit."

The old man and Curtis joined her on the couch. Lightning sat on a floor cushion. The boy continued looking at the photograph on the wall.

"That's my great grandfather, Bunun tribal Chief Raho Ari," Mrs. Ari said proudly. "He led a resistance against the Japanese colonialists. Refused to surrender. Killed Japanese soldiers who were trying to capture our people."

The old man smiled at the thought of dead Japanese soldiers. Curtis nodded politely.

Mrs. Ari ran her hands over her lap. "Excuse me, Mr. Lee," she said as she turned toward the old man, "we're so very thankful for the many times you've brought us sustenance, but please—"

"Drove by our old place," Lightning said cutting her

off, "there's two hectares of pomegranates where our papaya trees used to be."

"They've got mean dogs, too," Elephant said as she glided into the living room. She was eighteen, a year younger than Lightning; pretty, slim, in jeans and a L.A. Lakers jersey.

Mrs. Ari was embarrassed by the interruption. She took the top off an ornate ceramic teapot that sat on the coffee table. Elephant went into the kitchen and returned with a small pot of boiling water, a sack of tea. She sat on a floor cushion next to her sister and began preparing tea.

"As I was saying before, Mr. Lee, we're fine and your kindness is so very much appreciated but not necessary. The burden maybe is too much, yes?"

The old man fiddled with his tie and empty tea cup.

"I've a feeling this visit," she said as she reached over and lit the old man's cigarette, "is something wrong Mr. Lee? Pardon my directness."

The old man straightened up, smiled at the girls, and humbly said, "You'd be doing me the greatest honor if you gave me permission, if you allowed me to assist in sending your daughters to university."

Elephant smiled and looked at her mother excitedly. Lightning looked on, not as excited.

"Oh, my god. Thank you," said Mrs. Ari. "But the cost. The cost would be—"

"Don't. Please, don't be concerned with that. I imagine they scored highly on their college entrance exams during their final year in high school."

"In the top five percent," Elephant said.

"My good friend, Professor Kung, was a professor of

distinction at National Taiwan University. I'm certain he'll agree to assist and provide letters of introduction. With the girls' exam scores and grades, scholarships are a real possibility."

"Really?" said Mrs. Ari. "Taipei's so expensive."

"It is."

Elephant looked at her mother with anticipation. Lightning was getting more interested about the thought of living in Taipei, Taiwan's "Big Apple."

Mrs. Ari eyed her daughters with apprehension.

"I know Yohani works selling betel nuts and that she does it to help support us," she stated with embarrassment. "Betel nut girls get paid, I know. Get paid three, four times more than lots of jobs." She squint at Elephant, wrinkled her nose, and said, "I don't know what Jia's up to most of the time."

The old man wondered if she knew Elephant posed nude for a magazine. A long silence followed.

Mrs. Ari finally said, "If they receive scholarships, okay." She gave her daughters another hard look. "But if their grades falter or they misbehave it's over."

The old man and Curtis smiled and looked on as the girls jumped up and hugged their mother.

"Let's not have a party yet," said a beaming Mrs. Ari as her daughters continued to hug her, "nothing's happened yet."

The girls walked over to the old man, bowed formally, and thanked him.

7

Curtis worked alongside his grandfather from sun up to sun down six days a week for the next month and a half.

A change began to come over the boy, subtle at first, and then in a matter of weeks he was humming and singing happy tunes nearly every day while he worked.

The old man knew what it was—the boy was starting to "see." Nature and honest work were healing him. He was also reading the books the old man placed in his room each week. He'd finished Lao Ho's book of poetry, *The Old Man and the Sea*, *Macbeth*, Half the *Tao Te Ching*, and had begun *The Grapes of Wrath*. This pleased his grandfather.

Several nights a week, when he wasn't too exhausted from the day's work, the boy walked out into the warm night air and practiced chi gong with his grandfather. He worked hard trying to match the old man's movements exactly.

Curtis also worked with the women when they returned two weeks after the initial Irwin harvest to complete picking and packing the rest of the mangos. The harvest was bountiful due to mild spring weather and steady, hot temperatures. This delighted the old man, giving him bragging rights among fellow growers.

In mid-July, several weeks after the second Irwin harvest, Curtis again worked with the women and harvested the Chin-huang mangos. The old man continued to teach the boy every aspect of tending to the mango trees.

The corn he planted started to grow and flourish, and the boy could barely contain his excitement about it. On his day off, the boy usually slept most of the day.

On Monday in the third week of July, the old man bent down, scooped up a handful of moist black soil and placed it into Curtis's hands like he'd done repeatedly over the summer. He'd always received the same disinterested shrug.

"What's that?" said the old man.

The boy rubbed the soil between his hands and said, "There're no words for it. It's a feeling like—like home."

The sky and land and mango trees had taken hold of the boy. He'd taken hold of them. On several recent occasions like this one, while working in the orchard or tending his corn crop, he felt blissful. His soul rising up out of him. Beyond the reach of pain and memory and want. He'd become a perfect note in the eternal melody.

This feeling was fleeting, as the good tiger and the evil tiger continued their battle.

8

Mr. Hai Lee's library was his refuge—a never-ending flame illuminating a thousand adventures. It was a monument to his father, and after his father passed away Hai gladly took over as librarian.

One Saturday evening after supper the old man led Curtis into the library for the first time. He switched on two hand-painted blue lanterns that hung from the cedar ceiling. The shoebox-shaped room glowed softly. The boy gasped in wonder. After the lanterns, the second thing he noticed was a striking red tatami mat that covered the floor. Two bookcases ran along the walls.

"Please repose," the old man said, as he sat in an elegant recliner.

The boy sat in the other recliner next to a small rectangular table. His eyes scanned the bookcase opposite him. He smiled as he recognized novels from Bo Yang, Dostoevsky, and screenplays by Ang Lee.

"This was my father's and now it's yours, too."

The boy smiled humbly. "Any rules?"

"One. Return a book to the place you found it."

"Have you read them all? How many are here?"

"About a thousand. Read some of them two, three times. You can add to the collection if you wish."

The boy noticed his grandfather spoke politely, softly, with the same reverence he used in the shrine room or when he spoke to Mrs. Ari and her daughters.

The boy stood up and walked along the bookcase nearest to him. He turned, searched over the framed black-and-white photographs on the walls on either side of the door.

The old man turned and said, "My mother and father, the big ones on the right."

Curtis studied the photographs for a few minutes before returning to his chair.

The old man waved an arm toward the far bookcase and said, "A good book can render knowledge, truth, a moving experience. It can change your thinking. A great book does these things, too." He torched a cig, blew a halo smoke ring, turned, looked into the boy's eyes and said slowly, accentuating each word, "A great book also electrifies your perception. Frees your spirit. Catapulting you further ahead on the path of wisdom and happiness."

The boy smiled. He was captivated.

The old man continued, "It can change your life. What a gift! Same can be said for a piece of music or a work of art. A film. One must be open to allow these things to flow inside you. Then your own creativity mixes with these things and you release something uniquely your own into the world. There are many kinds of artists."

"You're an artist. With the mangos."

With a rare look of embarrassment the old man laughed and said, "I'm no artist." He took a long drag and exhaled. "I'm their fortunate servant."

"I'm sure they feel honored."

The old man looked at the boy intently and said, "Want to really broaden your mind?"

"Sure. How?"

"Continue to read the classics like you've been doing. The great works which inspire intellectual thought, freedom of speech, religion, press, and so on. Compassion, benevolence." The old man sighed and smiled.

The boy nodded and waited anxiously for his grandfather to continue.

"Also, read works about things you don't believe in. The Bible. The Koran. Marx. Works by some of mankind's worst villains; Mao's Little Red Book. Hitler's Mein Kampf. Ku Klux Klan literature." The old man waved a hand around. "They're all here."

"Ku Klux who?"

"Ku Klux Klan. White supremacist group in America. An institution founded on hate. Possibly the most ignorant, vile, inhuman organization ever formed in that country."

"Know your enemy?"

"Exactly. And, as in works such as the Bible, the Koran etcetera, it's wise to have this knowledge that's so widely influenced mankind through the centuries."

9

After supper one evening a week later, the old man and the boy were sitting on the front porch watching the sunset.

The old man went into the san-ho yuan and returned with a rectangular box. He handed it to the boy and sat back down in the rocker.

The boy opened it. He pulled out a new white T-shirt and held it up. The word "punk" was written across the front in Chinese characters with felt-tip marker. The boy sighed heavily and looked at his grandfather with disappointment.

The old man stared at the boy with a straight face, and then he looked down at the box.

The boy removed a thin layer of white tissue paper that the T-shirt rested upon and gasped, "Oh my god!"

The boy held up an authentic New York Yankees warm-up jacket with "Curtis" sewn in small script on the right breast.

"It's awesome!" yelled the boy.

"That 'hoodlum' T-shirt I gave you when you first got here doesn't fit you anymore, Curtis," said the old man. "I think this will."

The boy stood up and put on the jacket.

"It fits great," said the boy, and he ran his hands along the shiny black material.

"Now, there's my grandson," said the old man with a smile.

The boy rushed over, got down on his knees and wrapped his arms around his grandfather. The old man held his grandson tightly.

"Thank you," said the boy, and he began to cry.

The old man held the boy even closer as tears ran down his own cheeks.

Several minutes later, the boy stood up and began to walk nervously around the porch in small circles as he rubbed the slick material of his new jacket.

Curtis said without looking at his grandfather, "The girl got so sick from our persecution that she had to change schools and go to a psychiatrist. She had a nervous breakdown."

"Oh?" grunted the old man with a surprised look.

"I didn't have many friends. A group of older boys at school began to threaten me with beatings if I didn't join them in their cruelty. Extorting money from this poor girl. I was the one. I was the one who threatened her the most. Got the money from her. At first I planned that I'd later give it all back and tell her that these guys made me do it. But I was too weak. Then it was too late. She'd already left school. It was my fault. I can't forgive myself. I shouldn't forgive myself. I went to her house to apologize. Her mother screamed at me. Wouldn't let the girl come to the door."

The old man thought of the unmarked grave behind the house. "Fight it off," he said.

"Fight what off?"

"The damn stinking guilt," he growled, stood up and nearly fell off the porch. He grabbed the back of the chair to steady himself.

"Your eyes blurry again?"

"What do you think?" he barked. "Shadows are also coming in from the sides of both eyes."

"How long has that been going on?"

"A few days," he lied, and slowly walked into the house.

10

"Got a circus job," the old man said.

Professor Kung looked up from his bowl of stinky tofu at Ciatou Night Market. "Huh? What?"

"Sideshow freak. Between the Bearded Lady and Lobster Boy. They call me the Human Eclipse."

"What's he ranting about?" the professor asked Curtis.

Curtis frowned at his grandfather. "He thinks he's going blind," he scoffed. "Dr. Chang said there's a sixty, seventy percent chance or more he'll have full vision after the operation."

"Hangman's odds," moaned the old man.

Past the mob walking past, firecrackers and bottle rockets began exploding and whistling from the temple next to the night market's entrance.

"Surgery," the professor shouted above the deafening

noise. "Why? When?"

"A red house is what I need. Made love to a pretty gal there and saw cross-eyed for two days. So did she." The old man crossed his eyes and made a screwy face.

Professor Kung pushed up his glasses and snorted, "Like hell."

"Both my retinas are detached." The old man took a swig of beer. "Left eye's the worst. I see bright lights flash on the outside edges. Blurry vision sometimes. A few days ago my damn eyes started doing an eclipse. Shadows crept across a third of the way."

"When's the surgery?"

"Next week," grimaced the old man. "Damn hospitals. Needles and nurses. Enemas. The complimentary IV cocktail hour."

Curtis and Professor Kung laughed. The three silently continued eating their spread of stinky tofu, Kung Pao chicken, and Taiwan Beer. The boy drank bubble tea.

Almost anything can be bought at Taiwan's open-air night markets. A maze of vendors hawking Hello Kitty T-shirts, clothing and shoes, fake Rolexes, pirated DVDs, sex toys, libido enhancers, puppies, exotic birds, and plenty of food. There're fortune tellers, foot massage specialists, and snake restaurants.

The old man saddened. He looked toward the entrance through the horde. Taxis came and went on the other side of sawhorses used to block the street. Hundreds of scooters crawled by, many carrying three or four riders, all wearing surgical masks for protection against exhaust. A Korean soap opera blaring from the roast duck vendor's TV next door caught the old man's eye.

"Kimchi TV," he snarled.

"What about HBO and To Kill a Mockingbird and Cool Hand Luke?" ribbed Curtis.

"Magnificent." The old man nodded toward the professor. "The kid doesn't watch TV."

"Impossible."

"He made me stop. Don't miss it."

The old man smiled. "He spends nights squirming about Lightning."

The boy blushed, bit his lip.

"The prostitute?" said the professor.

The boy's eyes widened.

"No," the old man replied, "the betel nut girl at Golden Lotus Temple."

"Right. She whored a while I heard and—"

"All lies about her hooking," the old man snapped defensively.

"Certain?"

"Her father left a few years back," the old man continued. "The snake! Girl got real depressed. Dropped out of high school. Honor student before that. Ran off to Taichung. Met up with some jackals. Got a job at a 'talking bar.' Ever been to one?"

"Hell no!"

The old man laughed. "I won't tell Mei-lin," he teased. "Lightning did that gig for a few months. Made great tips. Sitting and cooing to the lonely men. Gambled a little. But, she was no whore."

"Heard she got arrested."

"Bluebirds found out she was a minor. Probably by a pissed off customer who wanted to go around the world and got turned down. So, some detective called her ma and got her back home. She did ten days I think. A half-assed juvey program. But, she returned to school. Graduated with honors."

The professor folded his arms across his chest, gave his pal a knowing stare. "Nice sales job, Mr. Hai Lee. Get to the cash register."

"In a minute. Lightning has a sister, Elephant. Good kid, too. But running with bad actors a little bit, but she'll be okay. Been trying to motivate them to go to university. Smart as they are beautiful. Lend a hand?"

"How big my hands have to be?"

"Big. I spoke with their mother. Told her I'd cover living expenses if they get in. They've sent their applications to NTU. They've got the grades and high college entrance exam scores."

"And?"

"They need scholarships. Full boats. You know how that crap works. Army generals and KMT officials bribing school administrators to get their idiot brats scholarships so there's hardly any left."

"Ain't nepotism grand," sighed the professor. "It isn't so bad." He took a pull off his beer.

"Hell it's not."

"Even if she has a 4.0, if National Taiwan University hears about the girl's shindig in Taichung it's going to discolor her and be—"

"Then you get out your paintbrush."

"Think I'm that good?"

"Yes."

"Get me copies of their National ID cards. I'll contact a former colleague and a few friends on the entrance board. Hope the girls' hopes aren't up."

"They're sky high."

The professor eyed the old man with skepticism. "A betel nut girl?"

"Honor students. Both of them. Mother lost their san-ho yuan after the snake ran off. Kid works the betel nut stand to help support the family."

"What did the other one, Elephant do?"

"Something wickedly ephemeral. It'll get lost in the wind."

"What's the mother do?"

"Seamstress. Works crazy hours."

"Uh huh."

"Try?"

"All right."

Professor Kung studied his friend with concern. "Your eyes. Going to be okay?"

"No problem."

The old man looked across dark rice fields as he and Curtis drove home. He was petrified the operation would fail, leaving him totally blind.

He had insomnia again that night. He sat on the edge of his bed, lit a smoke, closed his eyes and envisioned his mango orchard. His wife in front of it, her arms outstretched to him. He soon fell asleep.

Worry plagued the old man the entire next morning. He drove the boy to Golden Lotus Temple. They hadn't returned since the trouble with the gamblers shortly after the boy's arrival. The boy saw the beauty of the place this time. He was happy they didn't stop in the social area to say hello to any of the old man's pals who'd teased him before.

Prayer didn't calm the old man.

11

The old man, eyes covered with heavy gauze bandages, was lying on a cot in a room off the san-ho yuan's shrine room.

A day had passed since he'd returned home after eye surgery. Zi, one of the mango pickers who the old man hired, had brought the cot along with a wooden chair and a small bamboo table that sat next to the cot.

On the table were a bottle of prescription eye drops, two plastic shields to be worn at night to protect his eyes, a pitcher of water and a pack of Long Life cigarettes.

The old man chose to recover in this room because it was easy for him to go into the adjacent shrine room and pray. He could also smell the soothing burning incense coming from the altar.

Zi, the mango picker, was in the kitchen teaching

Curtis how to cook.

"Dammit all," the old man bawled from his room, "how am I, how could any poor soul have to just lie here like a bum? For two weeks? I'm destined to be a proctology class volunteer. An asylum lifer." He ran his fingers over the bandages. "Doctor Chang said I'm not supposed to lift squat. Don't do squat."

Curtis and Zi chuckled.

On the counter next to the stove were bundles of kale and cabbage. A butchered chicken, with head and feet, soaked in a bucket in the sink. Zi put the chicken in a pot of boiling water.

Curtis said, "The vegetables?"

"About forty five minutes after you set the chicken to simmer." Zi grabbed a stir-fry pan hanging above the stove, primed the gas, and poured sesame oil into the pan. Within a minute the oil began to crackle sending the delicious aroma through the house. When the vegetables were done she asked, "Can you remember all this?"

"He'll kill me if I can't," Curtis said, and ran his index finger across his throat.

Zi laughed. "Tomorrow's your test. I'll come back and watch."

The old man appeared in the kitchen doorway. "Good idea," he said. "That monkey'll burn the house down." He felt the edges of the door frame with his hands, stepped inside the kitchen and took a whiff. "Heavenly," he sang.

"Boy Hero, I can cook for you every day," Zi said.

There was that name again, Curtis thought. Again, he wanted to ask his grandfather what "Boy Hero" meant, but was certain by the way the old man slunk down after Zi said it that he was going to keep quiet anyway.

"Thanks Zi, but I want to do it," Curtis said.

The old man was relieved that the question he expected didn't come. The boy's eagerness pleased him.

"Zi, let's give the boy a chance."

Zi went home after lunch and told her husband, "Boy Hero fussed and bitched all during lunch, passed gas and laughed afterward. And he wouldn't let me feed him. Even after I gently insisted. Instead, he threw down his chopsticks and ate with his hands, making a pig of the table and himself. God. He kept going on and on about his mangos, and the glory of F.D. Irwin."

"Oh, he's a sweet old bull," Zi's husband said.

"I know," she said.

Curtis was washing dishes after Zi left. He heard his grandfather, who was back in his room, letting loose a tirade of foul language that could've slain a swarm of hornets.

The boy tentatively stepped to his door, peeked inside. His grandfather continued with his barrage of filth as he lay on his cot smoking. He stopped when he heard Curtis sit next to him in the chair.

"Before your drops I want to read to you," the boy said.

"What the hell what? My damn obituary?"

"John Muir."

The old man huffed and snorted. "I don't know if I deserve his words right now. Holy words for a miserable wretch like me."

"You've been quoting him and reading him to me. Come on."

The old man brooded. "Oh, all right. Go ahead." He blew a smoke ring. "Don't think about asking me the question on your mind."

"Boy—?"

"That's the one," the old man blurted.

They sat in silence.

"Hell with the doctor," the old man finally said.

"I thought you liked Dr. Chang?"

"I'll marry the pompous snob if I can see! Buy him a ring the size of his ego. Another ring for his ugly flat nose."

"Ego? As doctors go Dr. Chang's humble. He said your operation went well."

"To hell with hospitals! Damn nurse offered to throw in a complimentary enema."

"She did not."

The old man crushed out his cigarette and said, "Let's hear John Muir."

Curtis lifted the dog-eared copy of *My First Summer in the Sierra* off his lap and began to read. Thirty minutes later there was a knock on the door. The boy went to answer it.

Lightning, her sister Elephant, and their mother Mrs. Ari appeared in the old man's doorway. Curtis was behind them, his eyes tracing Lightning's curves.

"We've come to see how you're doing," cooed Mrs. Ari.

"Oh, my god," the startled old man cried out, and he sat up on the edge of his cot.

"Hello Mr. Lee," Lightning said tenderly. "El is here, too."

"We brought you some food," said Elephant.

The old man stood up and rocked on his heels unsteadily.

"I'm sorry," said Mrs. Ari. "Perhaps we've come too soon. We can come back in a few days. Better maybe."

"Please stay. How kind of you to visit."

"When do your bandages come off?" said Lightning.

"Fourteen days. Dr. Chang. He's a, uh, an excellent physician. Top top man. Said the surgery went very well. He's really pretty humble as far as doctors go, you know."

"Two-faced, ornery," Curtis whispered to himself.

"Wonderful," said Mrs. Ari. "Are you hungry?"

"Sure."

Later when they were feasting on the roast duck, barbecued squid and shrimp noodles Mrs. Ari and her girls brought, the old man asked, "I know it's probably too soon. Any word about your scholarship applications?"

"Professor Kung, I told you about him. From National Taiwan University. He phoned the other day and said all your paperwork's been received. An old colleague informed him."

"No word yet," said Mrs. Ari. "Regardless of what happens with that we are so grateful for your assistance. How are you feeling? That's what concerns us, Mr. Lee."

Elephant said soothingly, "What can we do to help?"

"Your kindness and compassion is overwhelming. Your visit to brighten my home is enough. My grandson does a pretty fair job looking after me."

The old man's filthy tirade just before Lightning and her family arrived echoed in the boy's mind. He chuckled, astonished at how fast his grandfather turned on the charm.

The old man had insomnia that night and the next. Shots of Kaoliang didn't help. On the third night he was still awake at 3 a.m.

"Kuanyin," he prayed, "how about letting me off with a heart attack? A monster that'll kill me instantly. Or a stroke?"

He lit a smoke and envisioned his mango trees swaying in the wind. Then, an image of the lone unmarked grave in back of the house consumed him again. He shook and trembled. Delirium settled upon him.

"Mercy," he cried. "Leave me alone."

12

Over the following two weeks, Curtis learned to cook well and diligently put drops in his grandfather's eyes each day. He also taped his eyeshields each night and removed them the following morning. He maintained the family shrine, going there with his grandfather twice a day to pray.

He also learned to drive his grandfather's motorcycle and took him back to Golden Lotus Temple three times. Curtis often prayed alone, asking Kuanyin, the goddess of mercy, to look after the girl he'd extorted money from, and restore his grandfather's vision.

Doctor Chang drove out to the san-ho yuan to remove the old man's bandages fifteen days after the surgery.

He'd called before he left the hospital. The old man said he was surprised and didn't know a thing about a house call.

"I thought I was scheduled to see you at the hospital tomorrow," he said.

A silver, blue and gold sunset adorned the sky as the doctor's car rumbled up the dirt drive bordering the mango orchard.

The old man heard the car, and twitched in his chair on the porch. He nervously sparked a cigarette. He bit down hard on it as he heard the car park in front of the san-ho yuan's courtyard. He lifted his left hand off his lap and patted the bandages covering his eyes.

"Easy," he whispered and popped a betel nut into his mouth.

From the orchard, Curtis saw the roiling cloud of dust rise from the road. He quit working and hurried toward the doctor, who was walking to the courtyard.

Doctor Chang was a country gentleman, feminine and thin, in a white jacket and tie. He turned as Curtis approached.

"How is he?" asked the doctor, and he looked toward the old man on the porch.

"Out of his mind," said Curtis.

The doctor laughed uncomfortably as he didn't know if the boy was serious. They walked across the courtyard and up to the porch.

"A house call?" said the old man.

Doctor Chang replied, "You're the first," and he sat down in the chair across from the old man.

Curtis stood next to his grandfather and placed a hand on his shoulder.

"Why me? Came out here to help dig my grave, did you?"
"No, sir."

"Sir? Now, I'm worried."

"I called him," said Curtis. "Told him you hate going to the hospital."

The old man growled.

Doctor Chang said, "I wanted to see the mango trees you've been bragging about."

"Sure you did."

"After speaking with Curtis I thought you'd be more comfortable if I examined you here."

"Well I am. Thanks. You'll get mangos out of the deal one way or the other. How many depends on the acuteness of my vision."

"Fair enough."

The doctor opened his black medical bag, pulled out a penlight, and put it into his shirt pocket.

"I'd like to alone with the doctor," said the old man.

Curtis walked through the courtyard and leaned against the hood of the doctor's car. He set his eyes on the two men on the porch.

"How have you been feeling?" the doctor asked gently, and he began to carefully remove the tape from the bandage covering the right eye.

"Like a son of a bitch." The old man squeezed the armrests of his chair.

"Please keep both eyes closed until I tell you to open them. After I remove this bandage keep the eye closed, okay? I'll ask you to open them at the same time after I remove the other bandage."

The old man grunted and wiggled around restlessly as the doctor began removing layers of gauze. As he finished removing the gauze from the right side of the bandage, the old man tightened his grip on the armrests until the chair creaked.

Curtis quietly walked back through the courtyard and stopped a few meters in front of the porch.

"I smell a boy," blew the old man. "I smell defiance," he continued, his voice straining.

The apprehensive boy crept closer.

Doctor Chang repeated the procedure for the old man's left eye, and after he removed the bandage, flicked on his penlight, held it in front of the old man's eyes and said, "Please open your eyes."

The old man took a deep breath and slowly opened his eyes.

Doctor Chang asked, "Can you—?"

"Left eye's blind," screeched the old man. "Right eye's blurry as hell."

He stood up, staggered off the porch through the courtyard. Curtis and the doctor ran after him. The old man fell, got up, and lunged across the dirt drive toward the mango orchard.

"Grandfather," Curtis called out as he and the doctor followed close behind.

The old man stumbled to the nearest mango tree, wrapped his arms around the trunk, slid down on his knees and sobbed.

13

It was late May 1944. Nearly three months had passed since ten-year-old Hai Lee was told his mother was raped by a Japanese officer—Hai's biological father.

The rice fields Hai'd planted with his parents in early March were ready to harvest.

Dawn snickered as the three entered the fields at 6 a.m. Heat and humidity slowly uncoiled as Hai assisted his mother in preparing the harvest basin. They fastened netting around six bamboo poles spaced two meters apart, rising two-and-a-half meters off the base of a circular wooden basin. A plank was nailed to the top of the basin across a meter-wide open space.

Hai's father was nearby cutting clumps of the thigh-high rice stalks with a machete and laying them on the ground. The boy and his mother would pick up an armful of rice stalks, carry them to the harvest basin, and with both hands thresh the stalks against the plank. The rice would break away and fall into the basin.

By nine, heat and humidity were on the prowl—fangs galore. The family had harvested a quarter of one of the hectare fields. This pleased the boy's father.

As he whacked an armful of stalks against the plank, Hai sang a traditional tune he'd modified, "Harvesting rice is never fun, bust your ass 'til the setting sun."

"Knock it off," Mr. Lee shouted. "Dan-dan," he sang to his wife, "clam the rascal up."

Dan-dan walked up to Hai, looked over her shoulder to make sure her husband wasn't on his way to discipline the boy and whispered, "Pray you won't find your real father."

Her words sent a jolt through the boy.

Dan-dan resumed threshing her stalks. "I heard you come home one night last week past two. And the week before twice. No, your Papa doesn't know."

"Are you going to tell Papa?"

"Of course not. You had my imagination going crazy. She rolled her eyes. "Do not go looking for him. It'll be the death of us."

"Okay."

Hai had continued to sneak out at night since March to work as a dishwasher's assistant at the Officer's Club at Gangshan Airbase.

Breaking his promise and disobeying his mother was excusable, he decided. His duty to save her honor was above everything.

The night job and the six days a week in the rice and

cabbage fields with his parents was murder. But, he remained resolute that he would find the man who'd raped his mother and possess the courage and skill to kill him. He was certain of it. Why wouldn't he be? He'd prayed each day to the goddess Kuanyin that she'd give him the opportunity to avenge his mother.

Hai kept his eyes and ears trained on a group of a dozen hotshot pilots and their superiors who'd always sat at the same table drinking and boasting of their flying skills and sexual exploits with local women.

One of them in particular caught his attention: Major Hirito Tanaka, squadron leader. He was thirty-eight, handsome, arrogant, and wore a magnificent *gendaito* sword that was unlike any of the other Colonial officers'. They were issued *kyu-gunto* swords with machine-made chrome-plated blades and *sayas* (scabbards) of brown leather.

Hai had never actually seen the sword that hung on Tanaka's hip. It was encased in a silver saya intricately inlaid with jade serpents. He'd heard the wonder of it from the dishwasher.

Tanaka and his pilots were drinking and crowing one May night during Hai's second month on duty.

The boy hovered near them as much as he could, methodically clearing away empty glasses and sake and beer bottles trying to seem inconspicuous.

As Hai took an empty sake bottle that sat in front of a captain, he overheard a new pilot of the squadron seated next to the captain say quietly, "Tanaka has sixteen confirmed kills?"

"If you count whores and dogs," the captain said.

They both laughed.

Hai slowed down, moved closer to the captain, gently rattling his bamboo tray of empties so he appeared to be working hard.

"Kanpai!" someone yelled, and everyone at the table drained their glasses.

The green pilot asked the captain, "Have you seen it?"

"No. You?"

The captain leaned into the green pilot, cupped his hand over his ear and whispered, "No one has. But I've heard it's the most gorgeous and lethal gendaito sword ever made. So sharp it can cut the head off a pig with one blow. There's a star stamp on the nakago to indicate it's a handmade Jumei Tosho, signed by none other than Masahiro, the renowned swordsmith."

"What'd he do to get it?"

"His skill flying the Zero was second only to the great Nishizawa. Tanaka's aerobatics were impossible, unbelievable. Among his twenty-three confirmed kills, he shot down four US fighters in one dogfight."

The captain took a slug of sake and continued, "But that is not why he was awarded the sword."

"Why?"

"He killed a dozen Chinese prisoners in the battle of Nanjing. They were brought behind the lines. Supposed to be interrogated. Tanaka shot them with a machine gun. He claimed they tried to escape, but they were handcuffed and in leg irons so it is told. Maybe the propaganda office made it up. Who knows? Either way, propaganda efforts have proved successful."

"How?"

"He's the most feared man on this island."

"Tell us what you two lovebirds are chirping about," demanded a drunk Tanaka, seated on the other side of the table.

Tanaka slammed his fist down, shaking glasses and bottles. Hai backed up against a nearby wall and stood quietly with eyes on Tanaka.

The captain answered with a sly smile, "The difference between Japanese girls and Taiwan girls."

Tanaka sat stone faced. The room got quiet. Then he grinned slightly, eyed the green pilot and said, "True?"

"Actually, we were talking about your sword, Major."

The pilots at his table gaped at one another nervously.

"You'd like to see it, huh?"

"I think everyone would, after all, I'm told no one has ever—"

"Insolent plebe!" Tanaka bellowed and stood up, thrusting his chair back.

The entire club grew silent and all eyes were on the enraged Major.

In a flash Tanaka unfastened the saya from his hip, and brutally beat the green pilot over the head and shoulders several times until he crashed onto the floor.

Hai flinched. He looked at the fallen pilot. He was an injured fly—crawling herky-jerky. No one dared to help him up.

Except for those at Tanaka's table, the rest of the club resumed drinking and talking, for it was common for Japanese officers to strike their subordinates.

Tanaka refastened his saya to his hip, and casually sat down.

He sparked a cigarette, poured himself sake, and announced to the table, "I've found Taiwanese women to be most extraordinary, but one in particular was the most memorable."

Hai's gut tightened.

"Here he goes," one of Tanaka's pilots moaned under his breath.

Tanaka smacked his lips. "About a decade ago," he boasted with a haughty smile, "I had the pleasure of deflowering the most beautiful chink in Ciatou."

Hai's eyes grew wide. He could feel his face flush. He thought of the many times he'd heard his mother referred to as "the most beautiful woman in Ciatou."

"Liar," whispered the Captain who spoke before to the green pilot.

"Dan-dan Lee," Tanaka said, and he smacked his lips again. "She was superb."

"Mother!" Hai screamed in his mind. "There he is. Damn. If I had a gun I could kill him now."

Hai walked quickly to the kitchen and through the back door where he dumped the empties into the tub by the dishwasher.

He said to the dishwasher, "I have to go."

"You have an hour left."

"I got a stomach ache."

"Why don't you take a crap. You'll feel better."

"I did. I won't ask for any food tonight."

"You bet you won't."

"I'm sorry," said Hai, struggling to keep his composure, "see you next time, okay?"

Hai started to walk toward the tall grass and for the first time the coconut palm grove in the near distance appeared foreboding.

He began walking faster when he reached the grove,

then he broke into a dead run for nearly 100 meters, collapsed, and began to cry pounding the ground with his fists. It can't be, he thought. That monster's my real father? He continued to sob. I'll get a pistol. Where? Don't worry, I'll find one. I'll hide it in the grove close to the club. When he leaves I'll kill him.

Hai stood up and calmed himself. Be vigilant, he told himself. Be strong. Watch out for Jap patrols. He cried all the way home.

The boy was startled when he found his mother sitting on his bed when he climbed through his window.

She lit the candle on the nightstand. Hai grew self-conscious and wiped away any trace of tears that might have been on his face.

This action did not escape his mother's gaze. He pulled off his shirt and threw it on a chair.

"Sit," she said softly.

Hai sat next to her. He thought of Major Tanaka and the scene at the Officer's Club. *I had the pleasure of deflowering the most beautiful chink in Ciatou.* The boy unconsciously clutched his mother's robe. Tears edged his eyes.

She gently stroked his head. "I understand your curiosity. Your desire to find your biological father."

"You do?" Hai said, realizing for the first time his mother couldn't imagine his plans to murder Tanaka.

"You can't confront him. You know that, don't you? Papa's right. We can't trust the Japanese." She paused and resumed stroking Hai's hair. "Ten years old and such a big bug already," she teased, "biggest bug I know."

The boy giggled quietly.

They sat in silence for a long moment. Then the boy asked, "Would you love me more if . . .? If I wasn't . . . if I was your and Papa's son?"

"That would not be possible," she cooed, and held the boy against her.

Hai began to whimper. She rocked him slowly back and forth. He grew weary.

"I'm sorry if I make you worry," he whispered.

Mrs. Lee blew out the candle, laid the boy down on the bed, and he fell asleep.

Hai quit his job as dishwasher assistant two weeks later, the night after he heard Major Tanaka was being temporarily transferred to Taipei for three months. He wouldn't return until August.

On the bike ride home after he quit, Hai told himself to keep resolute and that this change would work in his favor. It would give him time to perfect his plan of revenge.

Who knows, he thought, Tanaka could come back sooner. What if he never returned?

Hai tried to push these thoughts out of his mind and concentrated all his efforts on stealing a pistol. He knew this would be difficult. Taiwanese civilians weren't allowed to own firearms.

The Taiwanese recruits, he remembered! The poor young men that the Jap Devils are forcing to join their war. They'll have plenty of guns.

The scene of the neighbor boy who marched past his san-ho yuan months earlier with other deserters on the way to their executions grabbed Hai and wouldn't let go.

14

August 1944. Two months had passed since Major Tanaka left for Taipei.

Hai had sneaked to the edge of the coconut palm grove near the Officer's Club at Gangshan Airbase one night a week since the Major departed. Still no sign of him.

In July, Hai stole a Nambu pistol from a Taiwanese recruit named Kung.

Late one night in early August Hai stuck the pistol in his pants and rode his father's bicycle to the airbase. He crept through the coconut palm grove like so many times before and crouched behind a palm on the grove's edge near the Officer's Club.

He took the pistol out. It felt cold. He moved it from hand to hand. Ejected the seven-round magazine. It was full. Ran a finger across the top round. Popped it out.

Kissed it. Put it back.

"I'm going to kill my father," Hai whispered, the immense weight of the idea shaking him for the first time.

"He's not really. Responsible for my existence, yes. He didn't beat or disfigure Mother. But Tanaka took something from her. A terrible thing I can't understand. Something that has no word."

The boy began to weep quietly. He pounded the pistol on the ground.

"I can't go to the police. If I don't make him pay, who will? He gave me life. Life! If I kill him I'll be breaking many hearts, too. He probably has parents and family. Oh, Kuanyin! Help me! Tanaka doesn't know I exist. What if he did?" Fear surged through the boy. "The brute would probably have me killed along with Mother and Father!"

The boy slid the magazine back into the pistol, wrapped it in banana leaves and hid it inside the hollow of the rotted palm next to him.

August 19. In the hot afternoon Hai and his father had ridden the blue bicycle into Ciatou Township and bought provisions. Twine, work gloves, sesame oil and sugar cane. They placed the goods in the wire basket in front of the handlebars.

On the way home Hai sat on the frame in front of his father and chewed on a stick of sugar cane. They could see trucks coming and going from Gangshan Airbase entrance, which was only 400 meters away.

The boy's mind drifted to Major Tanaka. He wondered if he'd returned. Maybe he was dead? No! Scoundrels like that never die easily.

Air-raid sirens began blaring before they reached the outskirts of Ciatou Township. Shouts and screams came from nearby san-ho yuans.

"Over there," yelled the boy's father, and he stopped and pointed toward the eastern sky.

Four tiny black specks came into view against the deep blue horizon. They quickly grew larger. The droning of the engines were unmistakable, US Mustang fighters.

"Get on the seat," shouted Hai's father.

Hai dropped his sugar cane, hopped off the frame, and as soon as he climbed onto the seat his father sped down a narrow road toward the nearest san-ho yuans 100 meters away.

The boy held on, his arms wrapped tightly around his father's waist, his father standing up pumping the pedals furiously. People and dogs and chickens scurried everywhere.

Hai looked back. Two Mustangs came in low, a half kilometer away. In an instant, they were over the airbase, machine gun fire blazing. A bomb exploded, and another. Black smoke billowed into the sky above the runway. The sound of Japanese anti-aircraft artillery was deafening.

The other pair of Mustangs followed close behind, veering toward the hangars and supply huts. The Mustangs' machine guns spat, strafing the buildings and nearby san-ho yuans. They zoomed past, directly overhead, and the boy looked up and saw the star emblems on the undersides of the wings.

"They'll circle back," Hai's father shouted as they came upon the san-ho yuans.

A girl stood crying in the open doorway of the first san-ho yuan they came to. Hai's father rode up to the door. A woman's screams came from within. The girl pointed behind her.

They jumped off the bike and ran inside. The screams came from a back room. Hai followed his father as he walked cautiously down a long hall to an open door.

Four meters inside the doorway, shirtless and drunk, waving around a bottle of booze, TANAKA!

Hai scanned the room. A naked woman on the bed—crazy eyes—bloody lip. She pulled a sheet over herself.

Then, there it was. Major Tanaka's sword, lying on a nearby dresser encased in its silver saya inlaid with jade serpents.

Oh, I knew it, the boy thought. Kuanyin, thank you for delivering him to me. I know you did this for Mother.

The boy lunged for the sword.

15

The old man's right eye went blind three days after Dr. Chang removed the bandages.

His left eye had remained blind. Curtis phoned the doctor, who drove out the next morning. He examined the old man and told him he would never regain sight in either eye.

During the next two weeks the old man hardly ate, stopped making his usual wisecracks, and ventured only as far as the front porch. He sat there each day wearing sunglasses while he chain smoked and drank beer and wine.

A cane that the doctor had brought rested across a thigh. The old man brooded about his library, his precious books, reminded himself over and over how useless they were to him now.

He didn't practice his daily chi gong, and refused to go into his beloved mango orchard, even after Curtis and Zi repeatedly pleaded with him to let them walk him out there whenever he wished.

Professor Kung stopped by twice. The old man appreciated his friend's efforts of consolation and support, and it raised his spirits a bit.

The following week the old man was sitting on his porch late Wednesday afternoon. He heard a vehicle drive up. He set his beer down, grabbed his cane and stood up.

"Strawberry," he shouted, "where are you? Come out here and tell me who the hell it is." He muttered, "Probably some salesman or the KMT. If it's another bribe job I'm gonna drop my trousers and moon the bastard."

Curtis came trotting from behind the san-ho yuan carrying a hoe. A small blue flatbed pulled up in front of the courtyard.

"It's Mrs. Ari and her daughters," the boy exclaimed, "they're dressed up fancy," and he leaned the hoe against the house and hurried out to greet them.

The old man smoothed his T-shirt and tried to guess how many empty beer and wine bottles were waiting for them at the foot of his rocker. He couldn't recall the last time he bathed or shaved.

"Kuanyin, give me a hand here, would you," he prayed. He heard their footsteps approaching.

"Mr. Lee," called out Mrs. Ari as they neared the porch, "my daughters and I have come to honor you on this auspicious day."

"We received the scholarships," Lightning cried out.

Elephant shouted, "We heard yesterday. Full ones. Both of us."

"Congratulations," shouted the old man.

Mrs. Ari stepped onto the porch ignoring the empties, gently grabbed and squeezed the old man's hands and said, "We're so very sorry you've lost your sight, Mr. Lee. Curtis informed us last week."

"You're so kind," he said.

Curtis went to his grandfather's side and placed a hand on his shoulder.

"I should tell you about my daughters' attire," Mrs. Ari said and began to cry.

She motioned the girls to move closer, they obeyed and stood side by side at the foot of the porch a few meters in front of the old man and the boy.

"I'm sorry," Mrs. Ari continued, "my tears are happy ones and sad. Sad for you." She quickly composed herself and said, "Well, they're wearing special clothes in your honor for being such a compassionate and kind man. The likes of we have not known."

The old man choked up.

"They're wearing traditional Bunun clothing that I weaved. Would you uh, like to hear what the clothing looks like?"

"Of course."

"Okay. Yohani and Jia are wearing traditional full-length white garments overlaid with bright blue long-sleeved dresses. Cobalt blues actually, with red and black trim. There're many silver pendants draped around their shoulders fastened on chains woven into the fabric. They have braided headdresses. Yellow, green and orange. These outfits are only worn to perform tribal rituals on auspicious days and on special feast days, or for someone special like you."

The old man sat down in his rocker and beamed.

"Beautiful. I can see them."

"Girls," Mrs. Ari commanded, and the girls bowed. "They are bowing for you now, Mr. Lee," she said.

"Thank you, Mr. Lee," the girls sang in unison.

The old man was too overcome with emotion to reply.

"Mother made you a traditional shirt," said Lightning, and she walked onto the porch and set a shirt on his lap.

"It's a traditional hunting shirt men wear during our Ear Festival," Elephant explained. "Men hunt deer and bring the bounty home and young boys just learning how to shoot rifles try their skill at shooting the deer ears."

"Explain what it looks like," urged Mrs. Ari.

"It's really cool," said Elephant. "Uh, it's black. Mother made it, too. Sorry, Yohani already said that. With triangular patterns of yellow, green and orange that runs the length of the arms and across the chest."

Mrs. Ari said, "It's been blessed by the elders of our tribe. After they found out about your great act of benevolence, and all the food you've brought us this past year."

"Thank you," the old man said softly, a few tears escaping from behind his sunglasses.

He took a deep breath and said, "I'm so touched. Hey, would you like to stay for dinner? Zi, a friend, cooks for us now."

"They brought a feast, Grandfather," Curtis said excitedly. "I saw it in the back of their truck."

"We did," Mrs. Ari tittered.

"Huh?" the old man shouted, more surprised.

"My brother let us use his truck today," said Mrs. Ari. "To transport a wild pig we roasted for you. We also brought yams and traditional mullet bread and mullet cakes the girls baked."

"Zi," the old man shouted over his shoulder. Zi appeared in the front door. "You, my dear, have the night off. Would you please join my friends and me for dinner?"

"Love to," Zi said with a smile, and she started taking her apron off as she went back inside.

"Mrs. Ari," the old man said, "would you mind if I invited another friend, Professor Kung, for dinner? I know he wishes to meet you and the girls. As I said before, the professor was instrumental in facilitating their scholarship process."

"Certainly. It would be our honor."

Several hours later, after the joyful feast, the old man pulled Mrs. Ari aside and asked her to calculate how much money the girls would need for living expenses in Taipei each month, and assured her that he would wire the funds to her bank account the first of every month.

16

A week passed. It was August 19th.

Three weeks had bled since the old man went blind.

Curtis was sleeping in on a sunny Sunday morning when the old man barked into his room, "Wake up. We're going to town."

The boy jumped out of bed. Zi had breakfast waiting. Soon afterwards, Curtis drove the old man toward Ciatou Township on the old man's cruddy, sputtering Kymco 125cc motorcycle.

They rounded a bend several kilometers outside of town.

"Oh, Grandfather," Curtis yelled over his shoulder, "just ahead is a spectacular field of sunflowers that stretches for half a kilometer."

The boy remembered how he ignored the beauty of the sunflowers the first time his grandfather took him to Golden Lotus Temple.

"It's barren to me," said the old man, and he leaned his head forward jamming his thick sunglasses into the boy's back.

"Next to it another immense field with rows of purple, white, and yellow lilies glowing in the bright sunlight. You can smell them, can't you?"

Curtis slowed down, and when they got to the end of the lily field he turned around and slowly drove the entire length of the fields and back again.

The old man shouted, "Come on, we've got business."

"Come on? Smell them. Imagine what I'm telling you."

"Smells like dung," he snarled jokingly, tilted his head back, breathed deeply and smiled.

"Where we going?" the boy asked.

"Bleed off some steam."

Curtis throttled down as they entered the buzzing streets of Ciatou Township. People were streaming in and out of the open-air fruit and vegetable market that lined the narrow main street.

The old man called out directions and they drove down another street where an elderly woman was standing in front of her san-ho yuan placing sardines to dry in the sun on a long black net strung between four corner poles.

When she saw the old man she yelled and waved them over. Curtis pulled over and stopped in front of the woman.

"Who's that?" said the boy.

"An old friend," said the old man.

He got off the motorcycle and walked up to the woman using his cane.

She smiled and said, "Boy Hero, who's the handsome kid?"

"My grandson, Curtis."

"What happened to you?" she said, and studied his cane and sunglasses.

"Kuanyin took my eyes."

"Sorry to hear that. She give you anything?" The woman nodded and winked at Curtis.

"Damnation," muttered the old man.

The woman frowned. "What you been up to?"

"Been leeching the strawberries out of this kid."

"Uh-huh," laughed the woman.

"We need supplies. And the boy needs to blow off steam."

"Well, my granddaughter's here. You know Mei-chi. She's about his age. Please come inside for tea."

"Well, okay," said the old man, and he hooked his arm around Curtis's elbow and they followed the woman into her home.

The woman called for her granddaughter as she walked into the kitchen. The pretty long-haired girl came bouncing down the hall. When she saw the old man, she walked up to him, bowed solemnly, and placed her hands in his.

"This is Curtis, my grandson," said the old man.

"Well, come on," the girl said as she passed Curtis. "I want to show you something."

The old man became nervous as he knew where they were going.

Curtis followed the girl to a small room at the end of the hall. The room contained a shrine set up against the rear wall. A framed black-and-white photograph of a boy a few years younger than Curtis rested on the table in the center of the shrine. Orchids and offerings of fruit sat next to the photograph. A single thick stick of incense burned in an elaborately engraved dragon urn.

"Do you know who your grandfather is?" asked the girl.

"What?"

"That's him," she said, indicating the photograph with a glance.

"Huh?"

"He hasn't told you the story? Everyone in Ciatou knows it. He's called the Boy Hero of Ciatou."

"He won't tell me anything."

"Oh my god! I would love to tell you, but I think he should tell you himself. Ask him."

"I have."

"My granny has told me the tale many times. She was there."

"Where?"

"Come on!" giggled the girl and she ran out of the room.

Curtis followed the girl into the kitchen, where the old man and the woman were sitting at the kitchen table drinking tea. The youngsters joined them, and munched on crackers and sliced pineapple while the older pair continued with their light conversation.

The old man and Curtis said good-bye to the woman and Mei-chi an hour later.

The old man directed Curtis to a video arcade before they went to buy supplies and food. Curtis met some local kids and shot nine-ball with them. The old man sat in a booth and smoked while he waited.

Curtis had fun but was surprised to realize how much

he didn't miss his friends in Tainan. His grandfather hadn't given back his i-Phone since that first day, and Curtis had barely thought about it or his friends back home for weeks.

On the ride back to the house Curtis didn't say anything to his grandfather about the shrine or what Mei-chi had told him. Zi and Curtis carried the supplies inside.

The old man stood on the porch with a bouquet of white lilies from the market.

"Take me to the graves," he said, put a hand on Curtis's shoulder and they slowly marched toward the graves at the rear of the property.

Using his cane, the old man approached the lone grave, bowed, bent down, and tenderly arranged the flowers on the small unmarked marble headstone.

"Today's the day," he said quietly.

"What day?"

"The anniversary. August 19, 1944. I was ten years old."

"We didn't stop at that woman's house by chance, did we?"

"I always stop at that house on this day."

"Why?"

"And I always come back here. I stop there because she wants me to or maybe because I . . ."

"Was that your picture on the shrine the girl showed me?"

"Yes. People around here have been retelling the story of what they think happened on that day for more than sixty years. I've never told the real story to anybody, not to a soul except your grandmother."

The old man wiped his brow and said, "I've lived my

life behind a raven's wing. I'm tired."

Curtis didn't like seeing his grandfather this way. He seemed weaker than ever.

"What happened?"

The old man hesitated, and then he made a small apprehensive smile.

"It was a beautiful clear day," he said. "The Japanese had been here for what seemed like forever—long before I was born. The colonization began in 1895. My father, your great grandfather took me into Ciatou for supplies. On a blue bicycle with a big shiny basket in front of the handlebars."

"The same old bike you ride in the orchard?"

"Yup. I felt so tall riding with my dad. We got the supplies, and as we headed out of town the air-raid sirens sounded. It was a terrible noise. People were running like hell and screaming. I remember the screams of children and women.

"We heard the planes coming in low. American fighters had been targeting Japanese airfields here for some time. The one just up the road, Gangshan Airbase, was a popular target because of all the planes and fuel. The fighters had recently begun targeting officers' houses and Japanese command centers in Ciatou Township."

The old man became silent, got down on one knee and said, "We were taught that during an air raid you were to go into the nearest home for cover. We were passing the house we stopped at today. We heard a woman screaming inside. It was a different scream from those running for cover. It sounded to me like she was being attacked.

"Father jumped off the bike and ran toward the

house. I followed. We were met at the front door by the woman you met today. She was just a young girl then, about seven or eight. She was frightened and pointed to a back room. The room little Mei-chi showed you today.

"We ran toward the room and looked inside. A menacing Japanese officer, a major—he was in his underwear standing over a woman lying in bed—the girl's mother. He was agitated and waving an empty bottle of sake or wine over his head like he was going to beat her with it—the woman was naked and crying terribly.

"I saw the officer's saber laying on the dresser between us and him—in those days all Japanese officers carried razor sharp sabers. I grabbed it, pulled it out of the saya and ran toward the officer. As he turned I thrust it into his stomach.

"I'll never forget the look of horror and shock on his face. I don't know how I did it. He was bleeding like the devil and the woman was squawking and crying over him. It seemed like forever watching that handsome young man die. My father took the saber and was ready to finish him off if the wound I inflicted didn't kill him. If he would've lived, all of us in that house would have been strung up by the Japs. He died thirty minutes later."

"Oh, my god! Then what happened?"

"I'm so grateful that Father didn't have to kill that man," whispered the old man. "That's the only time I ever saw Father afraid."

"And?"

"We were lucky the air raid occurred when it did. In all the chaos and confusion we were able to sneak the body out of town. We placed it under some hay in the back of a friend's wagon. We cremated the body that night at a temple's fire chimney, big as the one at Golden Lotus Temple where we burn ghost money. Then we placed the ashes in an urn and hid it for years in our house. We only buried it here some years after the Japanese left."

"The Japanese looked for the officer, didn't they?"

"For weeks. It was said that he was quite a dashing ladies man and had several mistresses in town. But the town kept the secret. The Japanese also couldn't rule out that the officer was obliterated by a bomb that day."

"You're a hero, grandfather."

"I hate that damned word. I'm no hero."

"Why not?"

"The Japanese officer, Major Tanaka, was having an affair with the woman. Her husband had died, and she was alone with her children. He took care of them. He got drunk sometimes and roughed her up, but he didn't rape her or try to kill her."

"But, you didn't know that."

"Maybe the bastard deserved to be killed. Maybe. But not by me. That moment, that single error in judgment has tormented me every day since. That's my sentence for taking a life."

"You were only a little kid."

"To save the woman and her family's face, we never said anything. The woman created a story to make it look like I'd saved her skin. It went something like, just as he was about to run her through with his sword, I pounced on him, wrestled the saber away, and filleted him like a mackerel. People have been telling similar versions of that lie for decades."

The old man became silent. He nervously ran his hands over his shaved scalp.

Then he said, "Killing sent me to Desolation. These mango trees, this gorgeous countryside, that's what's saved me . . . that and your grandmother. Know what it's like to live with a lie for sixty years?"

"No," the boy whispered compassionately.

"It's a curse—a hell of a curse to brand a young boy with."

"Maybe it's not too late to do something about it."

Curtis was thinking of the shame he'd carried to his grandfather's mango orchard and how the old man had helped lift it from his shoulders.

The old man smiled affectionately. He bowed and prayed in silence for several minutes in front of Major Tanaka's grave.

"That's not all of it," he said quietly.

"What?"

The old man kept silent.

"Come on! You have to tell me the rest!"

Again, the old man rubbed his gnarled, weathered hands over his shaved scalp, leaned over and fussed with the lilies.

"Grandpa, come on. Tell me."

The old man ripped off his sunglasses and angrily hurled them to the side.

Curtis couldn't stop looking at his dead eyes—pupils milky as dove eggs. The boy retrieved the sunglasses, returned and kneeled shoulder to shoulder with his grandfather.

That calmed the old man, who cleared his throat, hesitated, and then spoke to the grave as if he were trying to explain to Major Tanaka, "Months before I killed you, when I was ten years old, my father told me that my mother was raped by a Japanese officer before I was born. And that that man was my real father. He said that he felt that it was his duty to tell me who I was. To tell me what I was, before I heard it from someone outside the family and rain more shame down upon us."

"You mean you're . . ."

"I'm half Japanese."

"Tanaka was your father?"

The old man waited a long moment.

Then he said, "I haven't told you the whole truth."

The boy tugged on his grandfather's sleeve and said soothingly, "Come on."

"It was different back then. The Japanese were our lords and masters. Mother and Father dared not try to get any retribution. They could have gotten killed for less. So they lived with this shame, and poor Father had to take it. And he did. My dear father, my mother's husband, he took care of me like I was his real son.

"Abortion was out of the question, being both extremely dangerous and illegal. I was an ornery kid, ahead of my years, and hard as the bark on a white pine from all the work I'd been doing in the fields since I was small.

"I was determined to find out which officer raped my mother and fathered me and kill him. I wanted revenge, damn it, for my mother and her husband's honor. There weren't that many of these Japanese officer devils around.

"So for the next year I kept my eyes and ears open. I got wind of Major Tanaka. He had a reputation for being a real brute and a bastard with local women. After talking with people and learning more about him, I was absolutely certain he was the cruel son of a bitch who raped my mother. He had to be. I heard him."

"Heard him?"

"To find the culprit I took a job as an assistant dishwasher at the Japanese Officer's Club at Gangshan Airbase. I heard Tanaka drunk, boasting he'd had his way with 'the most beautiful woman in Ciatou.' That's what everyone always said about my mother. How she was the beauty of our town. Tanaka said my mother's name. Her name! I heard it."

The old man shook his head, his face twisted in repugnance. "I stole a pistol. Hid it near the club. Would have shot him if I got the chance."

"So you got your revenge."

The old man kept silent.

Curtis raised his voice, "You got your revenge."

The old man began to sob quietly.

"Grandfather—"

"I killed the wrong man," he shrieked and tore at his shirt.

"What?!"

The old man put his face in his hands and sobbed louder.

After a minute he continued, "I was so certain Kuanyin threw all her luck on me when Father and I came across Major Tanaka the day of the air raid. It was perfect. The way we were there at the opportune moment for me to exact my revenge."

"You mean you, you . . ?"

"I killed Tanaka in cold blood. The real bastard got away."

"How do you know that?"

"Tanaka was a notorious liar we found out. Always lying about conquests with local women. It turned out the real scoundrel bragged about it at a card game in town one night when he was drunk. He knew all the details only the real culprit could have known. He had the necklace my mother wore the night she was raped."

"You saw it?"

"No. My father's brother did. He was a cook at a Jap officers' gambling hall. He told us all this just days after I killed Tanaka. My father's brother described the necklace perfectly. He'd seen Mother wearing it several times before. The devil who raped my mother was showing it off."

"What happened to your biological father, the officer who raped your mother?"

"We learned he shipped out a year or so after Tanaka's death. I had the opportunity to try to do him in, and probably could have gotten some help. I still had that pistol hidden. He was still in town. Abusing more local women. By that time, Tanaka's death continued to devastate me. I couldn't think about taking another life."

"What happened to Tanaka's sword?"

"Oh, god!" moaned the old man. "That terrible beauty. My father buried it the day I killed Tanaka. Where, I don't know. I've never wanted to know."

Curtis shook his head, his eyes filled with the sorrow he felt for his grandfather.

"You needed to know who you are, what you are, too," said the old man.

"Right," Curtis said, and he leaned against his grandfather, placed a hand on the old man's shoulder and murmured, "It's not too late."

"For what?"

"Redemption," exclaimed the boy. "Go to Japan and visit Tanaka's family."

The old man's face contorted like it was the craziest thing he'd ever heard. Just the thought of it terrified him.

"And tell them what?"

"Everything."

"God. I could never do that."

"Yes you can. You need to. You must. Ask them for forgiveness."

"Forgiveness," the old man whispered with disgust. "I forgave the culprit who raped my mother—my biological monster."

"What about forgiving yourself?"

"That's like trying to catch smoke with your hands." The old man stood up quietly. The dusky sunset grew faint. He torched a cig and slowly shook his head. "Take me back to the house," he said.

17

The old man had nearly mastered using his cane in the days after telling Curtis his story.

He continued to drink on the porch and still refused to set foot in his mango orchard. His moods were unpredictable. The pleasure and satisfaction he received from news of Mrs. Ari's daughters' receiving scholarships to National Taiwan University had nearly worn off.

One evening a few weeks later toward the end of summer, he and Curtis were sitting on the front porch after Zi made them supper. This was the first night that they had tried any of the boy's corn, and Curtis was anxious to hear his grandfather's verdict.

"That might be the best damn corn on the cob I've ever had," said the old man, "besides your grandma's, of course."

Curtis grinned. "Thanks Grandpa."

The old man's face was serious as he lifted a box that was sitting next to his chair.

"Take it," he said, and handed it to Curtis.

The boy opened it and found a beautiful old trumpet inside. "Is this yours?" asked the boy.

"It's yours now," the old man said. "I was a bugler in the army when I was not much older than you."

"Really?"

"I'd like you to learn how to play, Curtis."

"Why?"

"So your soul can speak."

The boy gently picked up the trumpet and looked at it with great admiration. It had obviously been well cared for; the brass gleamed softly in the dim light.

"A friend of mine will teach you. He'll come twice a week on Tuesdays and Thursdays after supper."

"I don't know if I can do it."

"You've been singing in the mangos all summer like 'an oriole from the valley.' You have a very expressive singing voice. I know you can do it. Just try."

"Okay." Then the boy frowned and said, "What about when I have to go back to Auntie's in a few weeks to start school?"

"How would you like to stay here? Live with me."

"Oh, yes. I love it here."

The old man hadn't told the boy his aunt phoned weeks earlier and said she was through with him.

"I talked with your aunt. I want to adopt you. Your new school isn't far."

"Let's do it," the boy said. "Thank you, Grandfather."

Curtis was filled with joy and relief. He savored the thought that he won't ever again have to face the bullies who led him astray.

"We have a surprise for you, too. Me and Zi." Curtis called out, "Zi," and she appeared in the doorway, walked over, and placed a book in the old man's hands.

He ran his fingers over the cover.

"It's Braille, Mr. Lee," Zi said.

"Muir's My First Summer in the Sierra," Curtis said. "Dr. Chang has arranged Braille lessons for you. We can get Braille copies of all the books in your library."

The old man gave a big smile. "Thank you," he said.

The boy went to his grandfather and they hugged.

18

A month later, on an early October morning, Mr. Hai Lee directed Curtis as he dug up the grave of Major Tanaka and carefully carried the urn containing his ashes into the house.

They removed the ashes and placed them into an elegant blue urn that Hai had recently purchased.

Hai Lee retrieved a metal box containing a black-and-white photograph of Tanaka with his wife and young son that were removed from the officer after his death. There were also four medals from the officer's uniform.

Several days later Mr. Hai Lee bought a new suit, asked Curtis to place the urn, the photograph, and medals into a handsome white gift box.

At 7 a.m. the following morning they took the subway to Kaohsiung International Airport and boarded a flight to Tokyo.

They were met at Narita International Airport by Major Tanaka's son, a man not much younger than Hai Lee.

Curtis was jovial, proud of his grandfather's courage and anxiously optimistic that the old man would gain peace from the visit. Visiting Japan for the first time and being excused from the monotony of school for two days added to the boy's happiness.

The men bought coffee and found a quiet place to sit near an empty departure gate. Curtis "took a walk," as instructed by his grandfather.

Tanaka's son was riveted as he listened to Hai Lee's account of the death of his father on August 19, 1944.

Hai couldn't bring himself to tell the whole truth, and fell back on the lie, the myth of the "Boy Hero" that the people of Ciatou had been retelling for decades. Hai couldn't say the things he desperately wanted to say. The thing he needed to say.

A long silence followed after he finished telling the lie.

Finally, Mr. Hai Lee said slowly, "I'm very sorry. I lied before. I killed your father in cold blood."

Tanaka's son sent his coffee flying, a few drops spattering Hai Lee's suit. Tanaka's son pounded the air with both fists, his face morphing between shock and grimace.

He quickly composed himself, sheepishly peered up and down the terminal and was relieved there were only a few passing witnesses.

Hai Lee nervously adjusted his sunglasses, fumbled with his cigarettes. A much longer silence followed.

"I stalked him for months," Hai continued. "I was certain he'd raped my mother and was my real father." Hai Lee pleaded softly, "Please forgive me," and he bowed his head and began to sob.

Tanaka's son paused, and finally said, "I am very sorry." Hai Lee lifted his head.

Tanaka's son whispered, "A terrible tragedy," and then his voice rose, "what a great and immeasurable burden on you all these years." He paused again. "On behalf of my family we accept your apology Mr. Lee."

Hai raised his head. His shoulders slumped. His sobs began to ebb. "Thank you," he said and bowed his head.

Tanaka's son bowed his head in return and accepted the urn and other items.

He consoled Mr. Hai Lee as best he could, and once Hai composed himself, the two men shared lunch in a restaurant near the airport while Curtis played nine-ball in an adjacent arcade.

The food was served, and after another long, uncomfortable silence, Tanaka's son said, "I think about my father every day, and wonder, what if?"

"So do I," said Hai.

Tanaka's son leaned forward, studied the lines in the old man's face and said, "My father fell short of being an honorable man."

Hai Lee thought about Major Tanaka's reputation as a brute and womanizer with Taiwanese women, and decided to spare the son from any more of this information.

"I've had trouble with my eyes recently," said Hai Lee, and lifted his sunglasses long enough to let Tanaka's son see his eyes. He paused, then he said, "I can see better now." He paused again and continued, "Perception. That word. I'm smitten by it. Its infinity. Like the gods. If ten men, or a hundred, or a thousand stood in a line shoulder to shoulder and an object, any object was placed in front of them, they'd all see something different."

A slight smile momentarily appeared on Tanaka's son's face.

"What you said before about your father," Hai Lee continued, "that he fell short of being an honorable man. Perhaps we're all destined to leave the shiny path of virtue, whether one's a ten-year-old boy or a decorated major."

Tanaka's son nodded solemnly. A small, forced smile appeared on Hai's face.

As they continued to dine, Tanaka's son ate in silence for over an hour while Hai Lee confessed more details concerning the officer's death.

Hai Lee stopped talking momentarily a few times, and each time the son pulled more of the black report out of him like a physician extracting poison from a snakebite.

On the flight home Mr. Hai Lee felt a sense of peace he didn't remember ever feeling before.

He and Curtis returned to Taiwan in the early evening. Zi was waiting on the porch when they got home. They shared a fine meal.

When the meal was finished the old man stood up and said, "Tomorrow, 6 a.m. wake up. We're going into the mango orchard."

Zi smiled, clapped her hands and jumped up and down.

"Yes!" Curtis proclaimed.

The old man stood up using his cane. He walked out of the san-ho yuan, across the courtyard and stopped ten meters in front of the mango orchard.

The boy hurried out and stood next to him.

Zi watched from the porch as the old man momentarily put his arm around the boy's shoulders.

He dropped his cane and kicked off his sandals, stripped off his shirt and began the graceful movements of chi gong.

Curtis followed his grandfather's movements exactly.

53156311R00074

Made in the USA
Charleston, SC
02 March 2016